The Skerge

By Reay Phillips

Never let people dash your dreams,

If you have a dream chase it,

Never give up on what you want , believe in yourself.

Thank you to my beautiful wife for always believing in me x

Thank you to all my family and friends

Special thanks to

Steve

Liz

Angela

Gillian

Cassie

Westney

Chapters

1. The great Hall

2. Riley

3. Bandits

4. Baldwich

5. The Skerge

6. The Emerald valley

7. The Crystal

8. Maze caves

9. The Battle

10. Reunited

11. The Skerge revealed

12. "Shoot the walls"

Chapter One

The Great Hall

"SILENCE!" said the great white Wolf, and a slow hush fell across the great hall.

The great hall was carved out of an old oak tree, with fires burning in each corner, casting flickering shadows across the many faces of the council who stood at the far end of the hall, raised on large stone plinths. The great white Wolf stood tall and proud with his armour glinting from the firelight. Behind him were the rest of the council members; an Eagle, Lion, Bear and an even bigger jet black Wolf, with a large scar over his right eye, and a permanent snarl. Animals from villages from miles around were also gathered in the great hall. They looked like farmers, blacksmiths, and their families and amongst them stood soldiers and warriors with weapons. All had gathered to hear what the council of the forest had to say. "We have asked you here today to address the growing concern we all have about the Skerge." Nobody knew who or what the Skerge was or even where it came from but for years animals had gone missing and turned into shadows of their former selves, barely recognisable anymore like they'd been possessed by a nightmare. "It is clear we need help and we cannot see another way than to ask the humans!" The great hall erupted into a protest, everyone shouting. An old Otter in the middle of the hall shouted: "But the humans are savages,

all they are interested in is power and greed and they should never be trusted again." We lived in peace once with the humans and we can do it again," chirped a twitchy

Squirrel in the back row. "Until they drove us off our land" roared the Lion, his saliva catching in the candlelight.

The other council members stood slowly, the black Wolf gave out a great howl and snarled and the hall fell silent once again.

Hundreds of years ago the animals and humans lived together in peace, each sharing the land equally, until the humans drove the animals off the land, wanting more and more for themselves and growing increasingly hateful towards the animals, until one day the animal council separated the world into two using all but the last of their magic. Unfortunately, they could not save many of the animals and most were trapped with the humans in the human world.

"We will use what magic we have left to send someone over to the human world and get whatever help we can find; we will need a brave volunteer." Everyone in the great hall murmured under their breath and looked at the floor. "Is there any payment for this task?" asked a voice from the back of the hall. All the animals turned to see who'd spoken and there stood an over-confident and smug looking Squirrel. "Payment?" asked the Eagle in surprise. "Yes" replied the Squirrel "Surely a task such as this will bring with it a large payment, shall we say two bags of gold?" "The fate of our world is at stake and you're thinking about gold?" asked the Lion. "Yes" answered the Squirrel. "Will anybody else volunteer for this task?" asked the Bear and again everyone looked to the floor and no word was spoken. The great white Wolf asked, "What is your name young Squirrel"Before he could reply the great hall shook, as loud, splintering-wood noises came from outside the tree. A giant, black rust-covered axe broke through the outer wall and in looked a hideous deformed Rabbit with matted hair and torn, bloody ears. "It's the Skerge, RUN!" screamed someone in the crowd of panicking animals. The great white Wolf pointed at what looked like a mirror leant against the wall and muttered something under his breath. Where the glass should have been was water-like. "Go now into to the human world." More of the Skerge were breaking through into the hall, the Eagle and the black Wolf ran towards the outer wall and started defending the other animals, both taking on two or three Skerge fighters, defeating them easily. The Squirrel didn't think twice when he saw the battle starting to take place in front of him and ran at the mirror, diving in headfirst. Both the Bear and the Lion headed behind the plinths and opened a door in the floor to a secret passage, shouting for everyone to come through it.

The Eagle and the Wolf were becoming outnumbered, so the great white Wolf instructed them to leave with the others ,whilst he stayed and held them off. As he drew his sword the Skerge stopped and seemed to back off almost as if they didn't want to confront him. Then from the hole in the wall whatever was controlling them appeared. At first, it looked like smoke but the way it moved was more like lava moving with a purpose like it was alive and he soon realised they were not attacking as it was he they were here for.

Chapter Two

Riley

Riley was walking through the forest with his two dogs, Bear, a golden Labrador and Lola, a black Labrador; He had just turned sixteen a few days ago, his mum had thrown him a party. Which only he, his mum and the dogs had attended. His father had left when he was a small boy and hadn't seen him since. He had no real friends to talk about, only the two dogs which he loved dearly. He tried to spend as much time with them as he could. His mum had bought them for him when his dad left to keep him company. He had grown up with them more his brother and sister than his pets.

He arrived at his favourite place, a large lake hidden by the forest. It always seemed so calm there and he and the dogs could spend hours just sitting by the water's edge. He picked a large stick-up, both dogs knowing instantly what he was doing. They jumped up trying to grab the stick with excitement. With a big swing, he threw the stick far into the lake. Both dogs leaped into the water with a huge splash. He loved watching them swim and wished he could be as happy as they were when they were swimming. Whilst the dogs were far into the lake something hit him hard on the back. "Hey, Riley no mates" drawled a familiar voice. Riley turned round and his stomach sank; it was Tommy Banks and his cronies. "Hanging out with your friends again, are you? Shame it's just a pair of slobbering dogs."His heart fell into his chest as he knew the dogs were too far away to scare them off. "Hello you big wimp!" the biggest boy said to him in a nasty voice.

"You not at home with your mummy?" Riley was frozen with fear and couldn't answer. The boys all picked stones and sticks to throw at him. Riley did the only thing he could - and ran. The boys gave chase until they had cornered him, up against a large rock. "We've got you now, mummy's boy!", as a stone bounced off the rock next to his head. "Your dogs can't even save you". As the boy lifted a large stick over his head to hit him with, a loud bark came from on top of the rock. Bear jumped at the boy, hitting him in the chest, making the boy fall on his back. Bear picked the stick up in his mouth and snapped it with his teeth. Lola joined them, the hair on the back of her neck raised and her teeth showing. The boy scrambled to his feet and ran screaming into the forest followed by his friends. The dogs turned to Riley, their tails wagging from side to side. "Thank you," he said to them, patting them both on the head. "What would I do without you?" He looked around and noticed he'd never been to this part of the forest before and began to find himself feeling lost. Some distance away he heard a strange sound like a clap of thunder, coming from within the forest. Thinking it may be someone to ask directions home, he went to investigate. As he got to where he thought the sound had come from both Bear and Lola became agitated ,until they got to the base of the biggest tree he'd ever seen. "I can't believe this tree is here and I've never heard about it, it's massive," he said. Bear and Lola started growling and barking up towards a low branch. "Be quiet" a voice shouted, and both dogs immediately stopped barking and stood staring at the branch. "You, human, come here!" said the voice. "Me human!" thought Riley, "who says that?" As he peered around the tree he couldn't believe his eyes, a Squirrel wearing what looked like a tiny half suit of armour and holding a sword, was standing there looking very angry.

"Are you deaf?" asked the Squirrel, "Come here." Out of shock, Riley replied "Me?" "Well, how many humans are there? I can only see one," said the Squirrel. Riley shook his head and rubbed his eyes "Am I going mad or are you talking?" "Of course I'm talking, what else would I be doing?" said the Squirrel. "Well, squirrels don't usually talk, to be honest" explained Riley. "Well this one does and I'm here for your help," said the Squirrel. "You want my help, what's up can't you find your nuts?" Riley asked jokingly. "No, stupid human I need you to help save my world, I'll explain more when we get there," said the Squirrel "Your world? And what do you mean when we get there?" said Riley. "See that knot in the tree there?" said the Squirrel. "Yes," said Riley. "Put your hand on it and all will be explained," said the Squirrel. "Yeah ok Mr. Imaginary Talking Squirrel, I'll do that, this knot here" said Riley." As soon as his hand touched the tree

Riley was pulled through with such force it lifted him off his feet. For a few seconds he couldn't catch his breath and felt like he was travelling at great speed, then without warning, BANG, he landed on a solid stone floor.

The room was dark and damp, and from the light streaming in through large holes in the walls, he could see that it was vast.

As his eyes adjusted to the light he could make out more details; he was standing in front of a large stone plinth with four other plinths behind it. Across the other side of the room, the walls looked burnt and as though someone had hacked their way in through them. As he walked to the edge of the raised stone floor he heard three loud thuds from where he'd just been standing. As he turned around he thought he must be dreaming as standing in front of him was the Squirrel, only now he was as tall as Riley and standing like a human. Before Riley could catch his breath and comprehend what he was seeing the other two thuds stood up, and to his amazement, it was Bear and Lola who were also standing like humans. Bear was tall and muscular like a boxer, in prime fighting condition, and Lola looked athletic, like a gymnast; both strong and healthy-looking, next to the squirrel. "What just happened?" asked Bear, and then his hand shot to his mouth with a gasp of shock "You can speak! Eeek so can I!" blurted Lola.They both started screaming at each other and jumping up and down. "Bear, Lola calm down," said Riley "I don't know how this is happening but you have to calm down." "Sorry!" they both said together. "Where are we? And what is your name?" Riley asked the Squirrel. "We are now in Silwane and my name is Archie,"replied the Squirrel. "So in Silwane animals are all this size and you can all talk?" asked Riley. "Yes! And I'm not sure why animals are so small in your world, and we do not like humans, so let me do the talking from now on" Archie said angrily. "We need to find the council members and they will tell us what to do,"Archie continued. Archie noticed the passageway at the back of the hall "they must have gone down here, come on," he said. The tunnel looked as if it was dug hundreds of years ago, with mold and moss all over the walls and water dripping down all around them. Every ten metres, or so, there was a flaming torch on the wall providing just enough light to see where they were going. "Where are we going?" Riley asked. "We need to find the Animal Council. Just as I was leaving for your world the great hall was attacked by the Skerge and everyone fled through this passageway, we need to track them down, shhh…. I hear voices!" Up ahead they could see the end of the tunnel with light streaming in so brightly they couldn't see what was outside. Then a voice shouted, "Halt who goes there?" "It's me Archie."said the Squirrel.

"Come out slowly so we can see you," said the voice from outside.

"Ok you lot stay in here and I'll go out and talk to him, if they see you they might freak out and attack you," said Archie. "Brilliant," said Riley, "I think we will stay here then." Archie walked out into the sunlight, and out of sight. "I heard other voices in there with you, where are they?"said the voice Archie had previously heard. "You know I was sent by the council to the human world? Well I did it and I've returned with one," said Archie. "What do you mean with one - with a human?" said the voice. "WHAT!!!" Another voice said. "You mean to tell me there is a human in there?" "Yes!"said Archie. "Are you crazy, it could kill us all?"said another voice. "No you're wrong it's quite safe actually it's harmless, not threatening at all, it's about as dangerous as a child,"said Archie. Bear and Lola started to giggle, "Oi, I'm not harmless!" said

Riley. "Looks like you are Dad, Archie said so!" replied Bear and Lola.

One of the voices outside shouted, "Human come out at once, and don't make any sudden movements."

Riley started to walk out of the tunnel slowly, putting his hand up to his eyes to try and shade himself from the sunlight. He emerged into a large clearing, his eyes blinking and taking a while to adjust to the bright light. As he focused he could make out two heavily armoured foxes, with spears pointing directly at his chest. He slowly raised his arms in fear and couldn't think of anything else to say other than "Hello!" Bear and Lola ran out of the tunnel entrance, barking loudly and ran in between Archie and the two Foxes "Whoa, whoa, calm down, Bear, Lola calm down!" shouted Riley. Bear and Lola stopped barking and slowly walked backward, hackles still up, teeth showing and growling deeply. "You would protect this human?"

said Archie, "Yes with our lives," said Bear. "But you are animals, you should hate the humans!" said Archie. "He's our Dad" replied Lola. "Wouldn't you protect your Dad with your life?"said Lola. "Well er, yes, of course, we would, what kind of animals are you anyway?" asked one of the foxes. Both stood with their spears lowered, looking a little confused."We are dogs!" said Bear "Dogs, never heard of a dog before?"said one of the Foxes. "Do you have wolves here?" Riley asked one of the foxes, in reply the foxes started pointing their spears at him again. "Yes of course we have! But there are not many left,"said the foxes. "But no dogs?" asked Riley quizzically."If we had dogs here, do you think I'd be asking what one is?" replied one of the Foxes.

Riley stood in silence thinking about the stupidity of his last question. Then it dawned on him.

"Of course, wolves and humans have never mixed in your world. So dogs have never had the chance to evolve. In our world, humans and dogs live together and over time humans have bred wolves into dogs" Riley thought out loud.

"Well if you're a part wolf then you're alright with me, we need more wolves about the place," said the other fox, shaking Bear and Lola by the hand. "The Skerge hunt the wolves down to try to make them one of their own as the wolves are the strongest and most skilled of all the animal warriors," said one of the foxes.

"There were thought to be only a few left and two are on the Animal Council" explained Archie.

"Actually that's who we need to find, we need to get this human to the council," said Archie

"I do have a name!" said Riley, but they just ignored him.

The two Foxes went on to explain that they were placed at the entrance to the tunnel along with fifty other guards to prevent any of the Skerge coming through. But never was there any sight,sound or smell of the Skerge.

"Do you know where the Animal Council has gone?" asked Archie.

"Yes" replied the fox; "They've gone to 'The valley of peace' to wait for your return."

The valley of peace was an ancient place deep in the mountain, where the Animal Council first used the spell to separate the two worlds.

"We will need to find a guide as I do not know where the valley is," said Archie

"Head to the village of Baldwich, you might be able to find a guide there,"said the Foxes.

" Thank you," said Riley to the foxes; but all he got back was a blank stare. Bear and Lola, on the other hand got a very friendly farewell from the foxes, somewhat like they were old friends leaving a party.

As they set off towards the forest at the far end of the clearing, Archie said "Baldwich is about ten miles away, so we might make it before nightfall if we hurry", and into the forest they went.

Chapter Three

Bandits

As the four of them made their way through the forest nobody spoke for a while, everyone deep in their own thoughts. Riley was thinking about why the Skerge had not come through the tunnel after the Animal Council, like the foxes had thought. "Maybe they were not some mindless monsters, after all, maybe they had a plan, maybe they were calculated in what they were doing," he thought. They walked in silence for about an hour until Bear and Lola both stopped and pointed their noses to the sky smelling the air. "What is it ?" asked Riley.

"I'm not sure," said Bear. "Since we have been here there are so many new smells. But this one I know, FOOD! There's also a fire over there," and he pointed to a thick patch of trees to their right, about two hundred metres away. They cautiously made their way to where the smells were coming from, coming to a large dense bush and on the other side was a small campsite with a smouldering fire with a pot of something bubbling, hanging over it, but no sign of anybody around. As they were all hungry and needed some food they decided to investigate. As they got closer Bear and Lola stopped and started growling again looking in all directions. Riley and Archie started looking around too but there was nobody around.

"I can smell three different people and they are very close," said Bear.

Suddenly, there was a noise from above and from the branches of the tree they were standing underneath. Three large figures dropped around them; one, a very fat bird with the biggest belly any of them had ever seen in their lives. He was chewing on something and holding a large axe. His armour wasn't really doing anything, there was too much of him to cover, so it just appeared like bits of metal hanging from him. To their right was a small, balding rabbit dressed in a robe, with an old piece of rope tied around his waist. He didn't look very confident at all and seemed scared. He was holding a small sword and shield that was shaking. In front of them stood a tall weasel who looked very old and weathered. As the weasel walked towards them they could see his features, it looked like he'd been in several fights, his nose looked like it had been punched too many times and behind his wry smile they could see most of his teeth were missing. He wasn't wearing any armour and had trinkets and all sorts of little shiny things hanging on a belt that wrapped across his body, over his shoulder, instead of his waist and in his hand was a large bejeweled dagger that didn't look like it should belong to someone like him.

The weasel looked them up and down and said in a slow croaky voice "Well, well what do we have here?" and he waved his dagger at Riley; "I've seen many things in my time but a human I have not."

"Are you not scared?" replied Riley in the toughest voice he could muster

"When you've seen the things I've seen and lived as long as I have then not much scares you, even a human. Now what have you got to give us?"said Colin the weasel.

As he came a little closer Lola ran at him and shouted: "That's close enough." Riley couldn't believe the way she looked, it was a controlled rage, very scary. It made the weasel take a few steps back very quickly; even making Bear jump a little.

"So, there are some things you're scared of then?" said Archie, with some amusement.

" Budududedthudduer hugtudurered!" said the fat bird, and everyone turned round to look at him with blank looks on their faces - as they didn't understand a word he said.

"Stop speaking with your mouth full of food Woody!" snapped the weasel.

"He said don't make the human angry Colin" said Hoppy as he backed away shaking even more than before". He's not dangerous Hoppy " said Colin. " Well even if he isn't, those two wolf-looking creatures look very dangerous, " said Hoppy; and with that both Bear and Lola used their new found presence to scare the rabbit a bit more, making him drop his shield and sword and run behind a nearby tree, whimpering. " Listen, Colin is it?" Archie said to the weasel "We need to get to the Animal Council in the Valley of Peace because this human is going to help them defeat the Skerge." Colin and Woody started to laugh "This human couldn't defeat me, so he won't stand a chance against the Skerge!"said Colin. "What do you know about defeating the Skerge?" asked Riley."We have defeated many Skerge fighters in this forest," Woody replied nodding his head in agreement, making crumbs of food fall from his mouth. "You've defeated Skerge fighters? I thought they were unstoppable?" said Riley."You've just got to know how to stop them"said Hoppy. "ARCHIE!! is that you ?" said a softly spoken female voice from behind them, and they all turned around to see a pretty young weasel in clean clothes with a shiny armoured chest plate, a sword in its sheath by her side, standing there smiling. "It is you", she ran over and hugged Archie."You know this squirrel Izzy?" asked Colin.

"Yes Granddad we have known each other for years, he's a friend." "And the others?" Colin asked.

"I don't know them. But if they are with Archie, then they are ok" said Izzy.

"I can smell something I haven't smelled before, and it's getting closer FAST," shouted Bear

"What does it smell like?" asked Colin "I'm not sure, it's like a mixture of mould, burnt wood , and rotten eggs!"replied Bear. "It's the Skerge , hide now" shouted Colin. Riley followed Colin up into the tree, closely followed by Bear, Lola, Archie and Izzy. Woody and Hoppy hid in the large bush next to the tree, the forest fell silent and they waited. The horrible smell that Bear had described became thick in the air, making it hard to breathe. Nobody moved. The only movement was in the branches of the trees from a light breeze. Riley could see both Bear and Lola's top lips curled up into a silent snarl and then he could see why. Walking slowly under the tree was a Skerge fighter. It looked like a Rat, but it was covered in mud, with a mismatch of rusty armour and was dragging an axe behind it, not really looking where it was going, as if sleep-walking. When the Rat was directly beneath them Colin nudged Riley and pointed: "Look, there, on the back of its neck," he said, quietly. Riley looked, and on the neck of the rat was a small black ball about half the size of a tennis ball, moving slightly as if it was breathing. "What is it?" asked Riley. "It's what controls them, it's what controls them all," replied Colin. The rat simply stood there not moving. Woody picked a large rock up from the base of the bush and threw it as hard as he could in the other direction and he could hear it land with a distant thump. The Rat instantly swiveled on the spot as if it had woken up suddenly; it picked up the axe, made a terrible screeching sound and ran off towards where the rock had landed. Three more screeching sounds could also be heard heading to the rock. When they could no longer hear them they all came down from the tree and out of the bush. "Well done with the rock!" said Hoppy to Woody. "They aren't the brightest are they?" replied Woody with his mouth still full of food. "What was that thing on the back of its neck?" asked Riley "It's whatever the Skerge puts on them to control them. I don't think they are actually bad, they are just in a kind of trance ordered by someone else. I think they all are and they all see what one sees so it's easy to distract them but if they see you it is hard to get away," added Colin.

"They can't see, smell or hear very well either, it must be something about who is controlling them and how many it's controlling, it must dampen the senses," said Izzy.

"We think if we could get that thing off somehow we could save the animal inside, but we can never get close enough," said Colin. Somewhere in the distance, they could hear more screeching; "We'd better get moving as they might be back. We are going to Baldwich, come with us," said Archie "Yeah, we need to get some food anyway," and off they ran.

Chapter Four

Baldwich

They got to Baldwich just as the sun was setting. The village was small and run-down and looked almost deserted. There were a few faint lights flickering in the windows. They found a barn at the edge of the village. Inside there was straw all over the floor. "We can sleep here tonight and then in the morning we can find a guide to the emerald valley," said Archie. "Grandad knows,"Izzy started saying. "Shhhhh child!"Colin cut Izzy off before she could say anymore. "You know where it is?" asked Archie "Well er yes er no," Izzy's grandad Colin, replied hesitatingly. "You have to take us there," said Riley.

"Don't tell me what to do human!" Colin snapped nastily back at Riley. Bear shot an angry snarl at Colin making him jump and look sheepish. "Stupid animal!" Colin said under his breath and he turned over and pretended to fall asleep.

" Let's all get some sleep and we can talk about this in the morning," said Archie and they all made themselves comfy in the straw and went to sleep.

The big, ornately carved wooden door was slightly open as the Kestrel ran into the large house. Sitting in front of him at a very grand table was the black wolf and across from him was the Eagle. Both members of the Council were deep in conversation. "Sorry to interrupt ma'am," said the kestrel. "Yes what is it?" replied the Eagle. "Our scouts have heard Archie has returned with the human," replied the Kestrel. The Wolf stood up immediately and barked: "Where are they?" "They were last seen heading for the village of Baldwich sir, with four scruffy looking woodland creatures and what apparently looked like two wolves."said the kestrel uncertainly. "Wolves?" said the eagle "Yes ma'am" replied the kestrel. The eagle turned to the wolf: "Flinn we need to get to them now". Flinn turned to the kestrel "Send two of your best soldiers to the village and find them and bring them back here safely." "Yes sir" cried the Kestrel and who then turned and ran back out of the room. "My men will find them Ruby don't worry," Flinn said to Ruby in a quiet voice. "I hope you're right Flinn , and what about these 'wolves' he spoke of, could it be true? I thought there were only you and Fenris left?" "I know so did I."growled Flinn.

Riley woke to the smell of food and the sound of laughter and sat up to see Woody, Hoppy, Bear and Lola all sitting around a fire, outside the barn, looking at something cooking in a pot. Both Bear and Lola's tails were wagging from side to side flattening the grass behind them. He looked around and could not see Archie or Colin anywhere, He got up and walked over to the fire. "Where are the rest of them?" asked Riley. "Gone off to find a guide," said Hoppy. "I thought Colin knew the way to the valley?" said Riley with a frown. "He says he's forgotten. Do you want some breakfast? It's nearly ready," replied a hungry Hoppy. "Mmmm yes, please. I'm starving."Riley replied,with a lick of his lips. As Riley sat down he thought to himself :"I wonder what they eat here? and I must not mention anything about meat." " What is it?" Riley asked. "Vegetable soup and some nice bread," said Woody, drooling as he stirred the soup.

As they all sat and ate the soup Riley noticed the village looked a lot busier now. "Where have all the animals come from, it looked deserted last night?" asked Riley. "jhfuwrehurrnuuinvoinvo, " blurted out Woody, showering half-chewed bread and soup everywhere. "He said they all hide during the night as that's when the Skerge is more active," interpreted Hoppy. Riley carried on eating his soup and as he looked around some more he noticed the other three walking back through the village towards them, without a guide by the looks of it.

"We couldn't find a guide but I have had a little word with my Granddad and he says he will take us,"said Izzy with a smile. "I thought Colin couldn't remember?" said Riley. "Well after I explained I wanted to go with you and it would be safer if he would show us the way his memory came back pretty quick!" smirked Izzy. "I also offered him a big bag of gold!" Archie said angrily.

They all finished eating, packed everything away and set off with Colin grumpily leading the way. After a good few hours of walking through thick forests and open fields Riley spoke: "So what's going to happen when we get there?" Archie answered "I don't know, I was not told. I was just instructed to get a human and bring them back, As I was leaving for your world the great hall was attacked by the Skerge and I left in a hurry so that's why the hall looked like it did when we came back through." "I hope they don't need me to be a warrior as I'm not,"stated Riley. "We can all see that!" Colin said under his breath, but loud enough for everyone to hear.

After a few more hours of walking without anyone saying anything, Riley spoke again "Colin, so if these things on Skerge necks control them; if we could get them off, do you think they would return to normal?" Colin looked pensive and replied: "I'm not sure, possibly." "We could try and see what happens" Archie spoke up from the back of the group, running to the front to join in the conversation. "I mean I'd love to give it a go". "We owe it to the animals to at least try," said Izzy trying to be part of the discussion. Colin stopped and turned to face the rest of them " Let me get this right, you want to find a Skerge fighter, sneak up on it, and just casually pull the thing off it neck?" giving a little laugh under his breath. "Well yes," said Riley "Something like that." "No, no, no, this is madness, it won't work!" squealed Hoppy and ran off into a bush, making the entire bush shake as he hid inside it. Bear and Lola stopped and started to smell the air and Bear looked at them all: "You'd better get a plan sorted quickly because we can smell one coming now." "Ok everyone hide, when it gets here I'll sneak up on it and take the thing off its neck," said Archie, hatching a plan. "What, just like that?"said Riley. "Yeah!" whispered Archie rapidly. "It's getting closer!" said Lola, as she ran into a nearby bush. Everyone found a good hiding place and waited. Riley started to think about how bad this plan was, but before he could say anything his nose was filled with the stench of the Skerge fighter.

Chapter five

The Skerge

A very tall and thin looking beaver, that looked like it hadn't eaten for a month, walked slowly towards them. In each hand, it held a huge sword, so big they dragged on the floor behind it. Luckily it headed straight at Archie who Riley could see sitting in the tree, poised ready to pounce, at the edge of a branch. The beaver stopped perfectly just underneath him. Everyone held their breath as Archie pulled out his dagger and dropped out of the tree. He landed silently behind it. He had to reach up, as the beaver was a lot taller than he was. Just as he was about to make his move the beaver flinched and made a strange noise, as if having a bad dream. Archie held his breath and didn't move just in case he made any noise. The beaver settled again, Archie placed his dagger just underneath the thing on the beaver's neck. His face screwed up in disgust as he looked at it. It looked like a fat, black slug with small tentacles stretching out around the beaver's neck, and it looked alive. With a quick flick of his wrist Archie cut it off, and it fell to the floor. Both it and the beaver were making a loud screaming noise like they were in pain. Archie stood there as if paralysed, not knowing what to do now. Woody ran over and, with his large foot, stamped on the thing Archie had cut off. It made a horrible squelching noise. Instantly the Beaver dropped to the floor, writhing violently. Its screams were hurting everyones ears; they had to put their hands over their ears to protect them. The Skerge fighter stopped moving as the darkness that once ruled over it was blown away, like thick black smoke in a breeze.

The beaver lay on the ground motionless; everyone came out from their hiding places, except Hoppy who stayed where he was, still shaking. They all stood around the beaver, and nervously Riley picked up a stick and prodded it. The beaver sat bolt upright and gasped for air as if it had been woken up from a deep sleep. They all took a step back while the beaver looked around ,blurry-eyed and breathing heavily. As its eyes focused and its breathing became normal, Izzy stepped forward and asked, "Are you ok?" "Er yes I think so, what happened?"the beaver replied ,looking confused. "You were a Skerge fighter and we rescued you"replied Izzy. "Thank you, It was like I was in a nightmare and I couldn't wake up" muttered the beaver. "Do you remember anything?" asked Archie. "I'm not sure, it's all quite vague, I remember being in my garden, then all I could see was darkness. I do remember always thinking about a blue crystal as if that was all I wanted" said the beaver, trying to remember what had happened to him.

"A blue crystal?" asked Riley. "Yes, it was like I was transfixed on finding it. It must be important." The beaver tried to stand up and was very unsteady on its feet. "Take it easy," said Riley. The beaver, now standing, realised Riley was a human and jumped back in fear " Oh my, a human!" "It's ok he's quite harmless," said Archie. "I wish people would stop saying that!" Riley said, a little upset. "What's a human doing here?" the beaver asked, still not wanting to be anywhere near Riley. "He's here to help defeat the Skerge," said Archie. "You'll need more than a rather skinny human to defeat the Skerge, I remember being in the mind of hundreds of animals, and they were in my mine,"muttered the Beaver,s till confused. He shook his head as if to clear it of the memories he had in there. " I need to get home to my family, which way is Baldwich?" the Beaver asked. "Go back that way" Archie pointed back towards the way that they had come, "Thank you all very much" and the Beaver ran off into the forest. They looked at each other smiling, and Riley patted Archie on the back. "Well done," he said, "It was nothing," Archie replied but everyone knew that Archie didn't mean it, and had been scared all the way through. They all turned and started walking again and Izzy asked Colin "What was the beaver talking about with the crystal Granddad?" "I don't know Izzy, but maybe the Council does," Colin sounded a lot more enthusiastic about finding the Council. Maybe he was,as now he knew that it was possible to beat the Skerge.

They walked for an hour or so and then stopped for food and a rest. Woody instantly produced enough food to feed them all but started eating it without offering anybody else any. They were all sitting at the edge of a small brook; Bear suddenly jumped to his feet smelling the air frantically "I smell someth..." But before he had time to say anything else a sword was placed against his neck. Archie turned to run and help, but he too had a sword pressed up against his neck. The two soldiers sent by Flinn had tracked them down and silently approached, without anyone realising. "State your name," the Black Panther behind Archie said in a clear, confident voice. "Archie?" he replied in a high scared voice. "And what are you doing in these woods?" asked the other soldier – a lean Cheetah. "We are taking this human to the Council," replied Hoppy and he pointed at Riley, his hand shaking. Both the panther and the cheetah behind Bear, lowered their swords. " I was held up by a CAT!" said Bear embarrassed, as Lola giggled next to him. "We have been sent to find you and escort you back to the Council in the Emerald valley," both the soldiers said proudly. "Brilliant" shouted Colin "Now we can leave." He picked up his belt and dagger and started walking away "Come on Izzy and you two we are off' he shouted over his shoulder. Woody, Hoppy, and Izzy didn't move. Colin stopped and turned around. "We are staying here," said Izzy "Yes I do believe we are better off staying with Archie and the human," said Hoppy looking a little more anxious than usual. "Why are we all being so noble all of a sudden?" Colin asked ,with an angry look on his face, " It's all ok living in the woods and stealing to get by Granddad, but this is something that affects all of us," pleaded Izzy. Archie stepped forward and said to Colin "If we don't stop the Skerge, there will be nobody left to steal from!" They could all see the realisation hit Colin, his shoulders dropped: "You're right, I don't like it but you're right." Colin looked hard at Riley

"You better be worth it," and walked off, grabbing Izzy's hand and leading her away.

Riley asked the Panther "How long will it take us to get to the Council?" The Panther replied with a purr; "We can't take the usual trails as the Skerge are looking for you. We will have to go the long way round. So two days, if we hurry."

After two days of walking through more thick forest and over Rocky Mountains, only stopping for sleep, they reached a dead-end. Bramble bushes as high as a house stretched to the horizon in either direction. The cheetah drew her sword and said: "Follow me, and fast, or you will get trapped in the brambles forever." She started chopping at the brambles to make a path through. They all followed her in. As the last of them entered the hole made by the cheetah, the brambles began to grow back behind them.

The deeper they went, the darker it got until the Cheetah's sword broke through to the other side and a shaft of bright light came through. They poured out just as the brambles snapped shut behind them.

Chapter Six

The Emerald Valley

As they all blinked in the sunlight, trying to adjust from the darkness, Riley spoke: "WOW! This place is amazing!" both the cheetah and panther smiled in appreciation. In front of them was a beautiful valley. The grass of the fields and the leaves on the trees were bright green and in the distance was the biggest waterfall Riley had ever seen, at its base plumes of mist billowed into the air. Beneath it was a large lake as blue as a sapphire. Snow-capped mountains towered into the sky and there was a small village in the distance. The Panther pointed and said, "The Council is in that village." They all set off in the direction of the village, mouths wide open in wonder.

As they walked towards the village through a field of long grass, the cheetah slowed until she was alongside Archie "You have done well bringing the human back, the Council is pleased" "It was nothing," he said smugly.

As they approached, Riley thought how much it looked like it was an alpine village, with beautiful wooden houses. Animals came out to see them as they walked up the cobbled street. At the end of the street was a large square with flowers and small trees at its edges. After that was a very grand looking house. Large, carved, wooden doors creaked open as they approached. The Council, led by the eagle, came out to meet them, all wearing the same white robes and looking very regal. "Welcome to the emerald valley," said the Eagle. "We have much to discuss. Firstly, you must be tired and hungry. Boris!" she shouted into the now large crowd gathered behind them. A rather plump looking Sheep stepped forward. "Please look after our guests," directed the Eagle. And he hurried off towards a building that said "The Fleece Inn" over the doors. "Boris will look after you this evening, we shall talk more in the morning, thank you," the eagle said reassuringly. They all nodded and turned to head to the inn. Woody broke into a run shouting "FOOOOD!" As Riley turned to follow, the eagle said softly, "Riley would you like to join me for a walk?" He followed her around to the back of the big house; there he saw the best-kept garden he had ever seen. Beautiful flowers lined the ornate path that ran through the middle of an immaculately kept lawn. "It's a pleasure to meet you, Riley, my name is Ruby" She spoke softly with an educated voice that made Riley immediately respect her as if he were talking to royalty. She was slightly taller than him and walked with grace and elegance. "A pleasure to meet you too Ruby", he said, nearly bowing to her, then looking embarrassed and turning slightly red. "Please do not take this as an insult, but you are not the hardened warrior I was expecting," said Ruby quizzically. "None taken, I'm no warrior. In my world humans are not like they used to be here," Riley replied. "Interesting," said Ruby, as she bent to smell a very large red rose. "I don't think there is any warrior in me at all, to be honest, I'm a bit of a chicken," Riley suggested honestly. "I know some chickens that are very good warriors," replied Ruby. Riley was going to explain himself but instead Ruby spoke again "I shall speak to the other Council members this evening. Tomorrow we shall see if we can make a warrior out of you!" "Er thank you Ruby, I will do my best, "Riley replied. "Go now and get some rest, you will be needing it I think" Ruby said ominously. "Thank you," Riley said and turned to leave the garden. Just as he was about to round the corner of the house, Ruby shouted: "Whatever happens tomorrow will be for your own good Riley!" He gulped and wondered what she meant by that.

He entered the Fleece Inn, to the sight of everyone sitting around a large table, in the middle of a big room. An enormous fire was roaring at the other side of the room. Food and drinks were piled up high on the table, everyone was eating and laughing, looking like they had all known each other for years. He walked over and picked up a plate full of food and a large glass of water. The Sheep from earlier was standing behind the bar, his round face with a large grin on it. "Could you tell me where my room is please?"asked Riley. "Yes sir, up the stairs, third on the left." Said the sheep. "Thank you, goodnight," replied a tired Riley."Goodnight sir,"said the smiling Sheep. The room was small with only a bed and a table against the wall. Out of the window he noticed people looking into the Inn and pointing. He sat on the bed, ate a few bites of the food and lay on his back, staring at the ceiling. He couldn't stop thinking about what Ruby had said to him. "I hope they don't expect me to fight tomorrow," he thought with a big sigh. He closed his eyes and drifted off to sleep.

A loud knock on the door woke him, "Hello sir, are you awake?" said a voice from outside. "Yes, one minute." Shouted Riley. Riley opened the door and staring up at him was a little Lamb, eyes wide with wonderment, at the human standing in front of it. "My Dad asked would you like these clean clothes? They should fit you ok I think." "Thank you, and tell your Dad thank you also, "replied Riley looking curiously at the clothes he was given. The Lamb made a small bleating noise of excitement and bounced off down the corridor. He got dressed and headed downstairs. Woody was laying asleep on the table snoring loudly. He looked as though he had just fallen asleep after eating too much. "Morning," Riley said to the sheep that was standing behind the bar again. "Thank you for the clothes." "You're welcome," the sheep said smiling whilst cleaning some glasses. He walked outside into the most beautiful day. The sun was shining and the air was fresh. He took a deep breath in and thought how the air here was so much cleaner than at home. "Good morning," he said to a few passers-by who didn't reply and just hurried along. He looked up towards the big house and noticed the cheetah walking towards him "Good morning Riley, beautiful day isn't it?" "I was just thinking the same thing" he replied. "My name is Ellie, I don't think I mentioned it earlier,"laughed the cheetah. And she held out her hand for Riley to shake, "Very nice to meet you" he replied, shaking it. "We need to go up to the house, the Council need to talk to you, and you need to begin your training," she directed. "I was worried there was going to be training," Riley replied. "Don't worry, it will be me training you. If it was Flinn doing the training then you should worry. He doesn't hold back. Bear and Lola are being trained by him." "He'd better not hurt them," Riley replied lowering his voice. "They will be fine. If they are descended from wolves then I can not wait to see what they can do," said the cheetah with anticipation. They arrived at the house just as Ruby was opening the door. She looked amazing as always in a bright white robe with a golden belt. " Good morning Riley, did you sleep well?" "Yes thank you" "Come in, we have lots to talk about." He followed her inside. Sitting at the table were the lion and the bear, both wearing the same robes as Ruby. Flinn stood looking out of an open window at the back of the room. His robes were the same as the others but black. Archie also sat at the table across from the others. Riley sat down next to Archie ."Morning"said Riley quickly. "Morning" replied Archie. The Lion spoke in a very deep voice" Archie has explained to us that there is a way of stopping the Skerge." "Yes sir" replied Riley. "Did you tell them about the crystal?" he asked Archie, "No, I forgot" replied Archie, looking a little embarrassed. "Crystal, what crystal?" asked Ruby. "When the beaver we rescued came round, he explained that all he can remember is thinking about a crystal," Archie said turning to inform all present. Ruby looked at the other Council members, they all looked like they knew something, but didn't want to say anything." Leave it to us, we will look into it" said Ruby in her usual calm voice.

The Lion turned to the other Council members, and as if to change the subject said. "This could be a turning point in defeating the Skerge." Looking very excited he stood and headed for the door. "Archie come with me, we need to pass this information on to everyone." Archie followed the lion out of the door. Ruby sat in the seat the lion had vacated. "We have been discussing why you are no longer the warrior the humans once were," The bear joined the conversation. "We believe you have forgotten what is to be a warrior, and with time this will come back," the bear said, trying to reassure. "The more time you spend in our world, the more you will remember." said Ruby. "We think with some training you might remember faster." She and the bear stood and she said to Archie "your training will start now, " and she pointed to the door. Riley gulped and made his way outside. In the middle of the square waiting for him was Ellie, and at the edges of the square, animals were gathering, as the word about the human, being trained had spread throughout the village. He noticed Bear, Lola and the others were at the bottom of the steps, the other Council members were sitting in ornate chairs, under umbrellas shading them from the sun. Ruby smiled as Riley walked down the stairs. As Riley approached Ellie she said "Don't worry, you'll be fine." Before they could get started, a loud voice shouted from the top of the stairs to the house. "I shall train the human!" Flinn was standing there now wearing his black armour and holding two swords. He walked slowly towards Ellie and Riley and the large crowd that had now gathered around the square gasped at the sight of the black wolf. "You are no longer needed Ellie" he said without looking at her, staring at Riley. "You can not start his training with combat, he is not ready." Flinn just growled at her and she stepped back, then walked off towards the stairs and joined the others in silence. Flinn dropped one of the swords at Riley's feet. "Pick it up!" he snapped at Riley. He walked slowly around Riley in a circle" I do not believe you are our saviour. And I don't like you!" "Well I think you're lovely!" joked Riley. A few animals in the crowd giggled at this including the bear from the Council. Then Flinn looked at him and growled again, he stopped immediately. Looking serious, Flinn shouted: "Defend yourself, human!" as he lifted his sword and ran at Riley. He swung his sword at Riley who fell to the floor trying to evade the attack. Flinn stepped forward and kicked Riley in the stomach. Both Bear and Lola stood barking loudly. Ellie shouted "Flinn that's too much." Again he just growled at her and she sat down. Riley got to his feet gasping for air, holding his sword out in front of him, "Is that all you've got?" gasped Riley. A few animals in the crowd cheered and then fell quiet as Flinn looked in their direction. Flinn started swinging his sword at Riley in a medley of vicious attacks. All Riley could do was hold his sword up whilst staggering backward, his sword being knocked from left to right from the power of Flinn's strikes. He dropped the sword and held his hands up "Enough, I've had enough!" Flinn just ignored him and punched him in the nose. Riley fell onto his back, his nose bleeding. Flinn stood over him and said, "This human is no warrior!" as he kicked dust in his face. Ellie ran over to Riley lying on the floor "You've broken his nose," she scolded Flinn. "I'm ok, it's nothing," Riley bravely replied. Ellie helped him to his feet and walked him over to the stairs. Two goats ran over as they sat down and started to dress his wounds. "You two" shouted Flinn "you're next" and he pointed the tip of his sword at Bear and Lola. They both jumped to their feet and ran into the middle of the square. Bear picked up the sword that was still on the floor. "You", Flinn said to a soldier in the crowd, "give her your sword." Lola took the sword, "Now let's see how much wolf you two really are." Bear and Lola ran at him, swinging their swords wildly, with no skill at all. Flinn defended himself with ease. Flinn used the dogs' attacks to move them into a position where he himself could attack. He ducked under a swing from Lola sending her spinning away. He then kicked Bear in the leg, causing him to yelp in pain. As Bear dropped to one knee, Flinn punched him in the face sending Bear flying backwards. Lola joined the fight once more, again swinging with no control. Flinn span around the back of Lola as she lunged towards him. He kicked her between the shoulder blades, she fell into Bear and they both ended up on the floor. "Ha!" shouted Flinn "you two are wolves?" Bear and Lola helped each other up "Come on Lola, we can do this, let's have him." They stood up and walked towards Flinn. This time they looked different; they each held their sword properly in both hands. They started to attack again,only this time they worked together, sending attacks high and low with accuracy and power. "They are remembering" Ruby said as she stood with excitement. Flinn looked shocked as he desperately tried to defend himself. The crowd started to cheer, as the dogs started to get the upper hand on the wolf. Lola used her sword to knock Flinn's sword out of his hand, sending it flying through the air. It hit a tree at the edge of the square, sticking in with a loud thud, narrowly missing a rabbits head, who then promptly fainted. There was a loud cheer from the crowd again. Lola then kicked Flinn in the chest, sending him staggering backwards. Bear held his leg and as Flinn fell over it, Bear followed him down with his sword at his neck, the blade stopping centimetres away. The crowd fell instantly silent. Bear leant into Flinn and said, "Don't you ever hurt my Dad again!" Flinn pushed the sword away from his neck, got to his feet and brushed the dust off him. He looked around at the silent crowd. "You were lucky!" he said and walked off in the direction of the house.

A great cheer came from the crowd, everyone on the stairs jumping up and down. Even Ruby gave a very regal fist pump. Bear and Lola gave each other a high five. Flinn entered the big house slamming the door behind him.

Bear and Lola ran over to Riley and sat down next to him, "Did you see us, Dad? We were awesome!" they said proudly. "Yes you were, you looked brilliant," replied Riley wiping some blood away from his nose. "Thanks, Dad, we did it for you, for what he did to you," they growled. Riley smiled and patted Bear on the shoulder as if to say thank you. Everyone came over to congratulate the dogs, " Wow," said Archie "you two were amazing." They all calmed down as Ruby and the rest of the Council came over. "We wondered what would bring the wolf out in you. It turns out it's the love for your Father." The crowd that had now gathered around them chatted, discussing what Ruby had just said. "This proves we can trust the human, we need to help each other now more than ever. Well done you two, that was quite something." The dogs looked extremely pleased with themselves. "Riley, Archie could we speak with you in the house please?" suggested Ruby as the crowd dispersed. Riley followed the Council up into the house. He turned to see the dogs re-enacting the fight with Izzy and Ellie, whilst heading out of the square.

Chapter Seven

The Crystal

They all sat around the big table again. "How is your nose?" Ruby asked Riley. "Sore, I think it may be broken," said Riley rubbing his nose gently. A smug snort came from the back of the room where Flinn was nursing his ego. "I'll get someone to look at it later," said Ruby. "We want to talk more about this crystal," said the Lion. "We think the Skerge are all controlled by a single mind, we encountered it when the great hall was attacked. They are searching for the crystal, as it is a source of great power." "Ethan, should we be telling them this?" Flinn said to the Lion. " Yes, they need to know" he replied.

"When the great hall was attacked they were after Fenris, he is the only one who knows how to unlock the power of the crystal" continued Ethan. "What can this crystal do?" asked Riley. Ruby sat forward and said in a very clear voice, "It has the power to merge the two worlds once again. We think the Skerge not only want to enslave everyone here, it also wants your world" Everyone sat in silence for a while thinking. "We need to find it first then, so the Skerge can not get it," said Archie. "Yeah, where is it?" asked Riley. Flinn walked slowly from the back of the room to join the conversation. "It's been lost for as long as anyone can remember, it is said to be deep in the Maze Caves." "Maze Caves?" asked Riley. "They are a labyrinth of dark caves, that lead deep underground," explained Ethan. "Many animals have sought the crystal and have never emerged from the caves"Ethan continued. "And you think YOU can find it?" barked Flinn. Who had now joined them at the table. "Yes, I think we can," Riley replied while thinking out loud. "How do you intend to succeed where others have failed?" asked Ruby. "Bear and Lola," he said, "they can find anything, they are used as retrievers in my world, they can smell out anything." "We shall leave it there for this evening, we all need some rest. We shall resume this conversation tomorrow," said Ruby. They all stood up from the table and said their goodbyes. Archie and Riley headed back to the Inn."Are they really that good?" asked Archie. "Trust me, they can find it,"Riley said confidently.When they entered the Inn a party was in full swing. In the middle, Bear and Lola looked in their element running through every detail of today's events in great detail. Archie went to join the crowd gathered around the dogs, Riley thought it was best to leave them all to it. As he headed upstairs to his room Bear came running over, "Are you not joining us Dad?"

"No Bear, I'm tired, you enjoy yourself you deserve it.2 "Ok Dad see you tomorrow" and he bounded back into the crowd to a big cheer. Riley lay on his bed exhausted, his nose throbbing. He could hear the cheers from the party downstairs as he drifted off to sleep.

He was woken abruptly by the sound of shouting from the street. It was still dark out and the burning torches held by whoever was outside were illuminating his room. He opened the window and a small group had surrounded two animals, his view was obstructed by a tree so he couldn't see who it was. Ellie and the black panther came running down the street, closely followed by Flinn, all looking anxious. The crowd parted as they got closer, he could now make out the two figures as the foxes, from the end of the tunnel to the Great Hall. They were in a terrible state, looking petrified. "What happened?" asked Flinn. It was the first time Riley had ever seen the wolf looking anything other than angry; he looked scared and concerned for the foxes. "Skerge fighters sir, lots of them," said one fox as he fell to the floor, exhausted. The other fox went on "They poured through the tunnel sir, we tried to stop them but there were too many. We headed to Baldwich to warn them but we were too late, they didn't stand a chance, sir."

The crowd around them started to panic. "Calm down everyone!" said Flinn and they all fell silent. "Ellie, you and Ben go and scout the area, keep a safe distance and stay out of trouble." "Yes, sir". Both the cheetah and the black panther shot off in the direction of the brambles, disappearing silently into the darkness. "Everyone, go back to your homes, we are quite safe here," said Flinn, as he glanced up at Riley looking worried. He ran off at speed back towards the big house.

Riley sat on the bed, his mind racing at what he'd just seen. "Shall I go and see if they need my help?" he said to himself "No, don't be stupid, they don't need my help!" He lay back on the bed, his head filled with images of the animals of Baldwich being overwhelmed by the Skerge. He shivered with fear; "Those poor animals!" he said to himself, drifting off into a restless sleep. A loud knock on the door woke him; "You're requested at the house," said an abrupt voice from outside. He heard footsteps run off as they left. He made his way up to the house, joining the others on his way. Everyone had gathered at the foot of the steps to the big house. Archie could hear worried questions being asked by animals in the crowd. He made his way up the steps, two large rams looking very mean, in full armour, were guarding the door, each holding a massive spear. Inside, the Council were in deep conversation. Bear, Lola, Colin, Archie and Izzy were all sitting at the table.

He could see Ellie and Ben at the back of the room explaining something to Flinn; they both looked dirty and very tired. He sat down at the table next to Bear. Flinn finished talking to Ellie and walked over to the table. Riley looked over at Ellie to see if she was ok, she gave him a nod as if to say; "Yes!" Flinn bent down next to Ruby and whispered to her, he then moved behind her and stood looking around the room, the stern look on his face once more. Ruby cleared her throat, "Due to the recent events it is clear that we need to take action, Flinn will lead a team to retrieve the crystal before the Skerge can find it. It is of the greatest importance that we succeed in this task." Flinn stepped forward once more "Ellie, take Bear and Lola to the blacksmith's, get them fitted with some armour, the rest of you get ready, we leave in three hours; Riley you stay here." He looked at Riley and his top lip curled up "You'll be safe here!" "But I want to come, I can help,"

Riley appealed. "You would put the rest of us in danger, you stay here!" Flinn snarled. Flinn left the room followed by Ellie and the two dogs. Ruby looked at him and made a gesture with her hand to stay where he was. The room emptied in silence as everyone went to ready themselves. "I can help I'm sure of it," Riley said to Ruby. "I am sure you can, and will. I believe you are here for a reason, and that reason will soon be apparent, I shall talk to Flinn. Go to the blacksmith's and get some armour," Ruby whispered. "Thank you Ruby, I won't let you down," Riley whispered back. He ran out of the house after Ellie and the dogs. "For all our sakes I hope you don't!" she thought. "Dad!" said both Bear and Lola, as Riley joined them at the blacksmith's. "What are you doing here?" asked Ellie, "Ruby told me to get some armour, as I'll be joining you on the journey". As Ellie was opening her mouth to speak,

Riley stopped her; "It is ok. She is going to speak to Flinn".

She smiled "Right then, let's get your armour sorted." The blacksmith's shop was dark and smoky. A large fire burned in the corner, bits of metal sticking out of it. There were suits of armour, of all shapes and sizes, hanging on the walls. A large rack of swords and axes stood at the far end, next to it sat a huge goat hitting a piece of red-hot metal with a hammer. He dipped the metal into a bucket of water and steam filled the room, with a loud hissing sound. "What do you want?" he asked in a deep voice. He was built like the side of a house, wider than he was tall, thick with muscle. "We have come for some armour please Frank," said Ellie. "Armour eh?" said Frank thoughtfully. Bear and Lola were looking at all the suits on the walls. "You're the two wolf dogs everyone is talking about?" Frank queried. They turned and said together "Yes that's us. "Frank made a loud huff noise like the pair didn't impress him. "I've got something special for you two, if you're as good as everyone is saying, you will need some armour that can keep up." "Brilliant!" said Bear excitedly. Frank pulled out a suit that resembled the armour worn by a Samurai. "This is a new suit of armour that I have been working on; it is as strong as steel, but nowhere near as heavy, perfect for a fast swordsman." "Could you make three suits in the next two hours?" asked Ellie urgently. "Three? Who is the other for? "Frank sounded confused. Ellie pointed at Riley who was still standing in the doorway. "The human?" asked Frank with a laugh, "I heard he couldn't fight?" "Not yet but we need to be ready for when he can, He will be the best warrior we have," defended Ellie. "Thanks!" said Riley as he walked over to them. "I can do the three suits but not in two hours," stated Frank. Flinn says we need this armour for when we leave"

Lola said challengingly. "Oh, he did, did he? Well if he has a problem, tell him to come and see me. Ha, Mr grumpy," he said winking at Bear and Lola, who joined in with him laughing. "Thank you, Frank, we shall be back later to collect them," said Ellie. Frank just waved at them as he turned away to start work on the armour.

They walked back to the Inn and Ellie told them to get some food and a little rest, she would come and get them when the armour was ready.

They walked in to find everyone at the table, eating; Woody, as usual, had an enormous pile of food in front of him. Everyone was quiet, thinking about what they were about to do. Riley sat down next to Izzy and Archie, "You two ok?" he asked, "yes, thank you, just a little worried about this crystal," said Izzy. "I'm sure we will be fine, with a bit of luck we can find it and be out of there before the Skerge even know we have it" Riley said trying to reassure Izzy. "Let's hope so," said Izzy. They were just finishing their food as Ellie walked through the door, "Riley, Bear, Lola come on, your armour is ready," she said, turning around and heading back outside as they stood up from the table. "I can't wait to get our new armour," Bear said to Lola as they walked to the blacksmith's. Frank was just hanging the last of their suits on the wall as they walked in. "There you go, three of the best suits of armour I have ever made." He looked at them with pride, wiping his hands on an old cloth. They were all identical, matt black with red piping around the edges. They looked just like those Riley had seen in the films; Japanese warriors would wear them into battle. "Can we try them on please?" asked Lola. "Why of course you can, you will need to put these on first." He handed them all a thick, padded undergarment. It was like an all-in-one Tshirt and shorts. "This will make the suit more comfortable to wear," said Frank with experience. "Thanks," said Bear, and they all put them on. "Bear this one is yours," he gave Bear the biggest suit, then gave Lola hers, and Riley's was the smallest. They all fitted perfectly, and they looked amazing. "Well at least you look like a warrior Dad!" said Bear laughing. "Thanks!" Riley answered sarcastically. He looked down at his Nike trainers and wondered if the Samurai had worn the same. "I made these swords years before I made the armour, but they should be perfect. They are made out of a metal only found in our world. They are strong, light and extremely sharp. I sadly only had enough to make three swords," said Frank looking on with pleasure at his final products. They were very similar to the swords carried by a Samurai. "You have outdone yourself, this time, Frank, I am almost jealous," said Ellie. "Well don't be. I have a new weapon for you too." He held out the most beautiful sword. It was long and thin, with engravings all the way up the blade. The handle was gold and it was wrapped in plush red material. "I was saving this one for a special occasion, and it looks like this is it" said Frank, smiling but worried. "Thank you, Frank, it's amazing," Ellie examined her sword in admiration.

They headed up to the big house feeling energised by their new armour. Animals came out to look at them, pointing at something none of them had ever seen before. As they got to the steps up to the house, Woody and Hoppy were waiting for them. "Izzy told us what you were planning on doing, and we want to join you," Woody said, without any food in his mouth for once. Even Hoppy looked like he actually wanted to go. They went in the house together, everyone was there, quiet and ready for the task that was ahead of them. Izzy and Colin were at the table, Izzy's armour shining as if she'd just cleaned it. Colin, on the other hand, looked as scruffy as usual. Ellie and Ben were also at the table; they looked fresh again, ready for anything. Ellie was deep in conversation with Archie; he stopped talking when he noticed the armour Riley and the dogs were wearing. He walked over to Riley staring all the way. "That looks amazing, how's it feel?" he asked Riley as he gently banged on the chest of Riley's armour with his fist. "It feels good thanks, it is so light I don't know I'm wearing any armour, "Riley replied with a grin. Archie nodded his head in appreciation and joined Ellie at the table again. Ruby and Flinn entered through a door at the back of the room. Ruby sat at the head of the table and Flinn stood just behind her again. "I see we have a few more volunteers joining us!" nodding towards Woody and Hoppy, who courteously nodded back. "We will be setting off immediately to recover the crystal, I thank all of you for joining the quest. Please know this will be fraught with danger, there is no disgrace in backing out, "announced Flinn. Woody grabbed Hoppy's arm to stop him leaving, Hoppy did not move and just looked at Woody, a little disgusted. "We will head for the Maze Caves," said Flinn stepping forward. "At no time will anyone engage any Skerge fighter we come across; we do not want them to realise what we are doing. If you see one, hide until it goes away. Once we reach the caves we will come up with a plan to retrieve the crystal. Does everyone understand?" asked Flinn. Everyone nodded. "Any questions? No? Ok, let's go," Flinn said as he walked out.

They all made their way outside, where a large crowd had gathered at the foot of the steps. They started to cheer as they walked past. Flowers were being tossed in the air and shouts of "Good Luck!" could be heard. They could still hear the faint cheers as they all reached the bramble wall;

Flinn stopped past the brambles, "we are no longer safe, we work as a team, stay together, Bear, Lola you take point!" They looked at him confused. "You go in front!" he explained. They both nodded as they realised what he meant. "The rest of you be vigilant, remember no heroics we need to get there unnoticed," Flinn reminded them. Ellie and Ben hacked at the brambles and started to walk through, with everyone following closely behind. Riley turned to take a last look at the beautiful valley and sighed, then ran through. He jumped out of the other side, just as the brambles snapped close behind him. Everyone was stood still on the other side, weapons at the ready. "What's wrong?" he asked. "Shh, Bear has got something," Ben said. In front, Bear and Lola were sniffing at the air both holding one hand out behind them as if to say "stay there!" Nobody moved until Bear broke the silence, "There is a faint smell of the Skerge, we should be ok to carry on."

They all set off again in silence.

Chapter Eight

The Maze Caves

Ruby joined Riley at the back of the group as they walked deep into the forest. Up front Bear and Lola looked in their element, Flinn, Ellie and Ben followed closely behind, watching the two dogs intently. They kept off the paths and stayed in the shadows so as not to attract any attention. After hours of walking and not coming across anyone, the group started to relax a little. All apart from Flinn who remained vigilant as ever at the front. "We need to find a place to camp Flinn," said Archie "The Skerge mostly scouts at night, that's why we haven't seen any yet." Flinn didn't look happy about stopping but knew Archie was right. "Everyone search somewhere to camp, somewhere hidden if possible," Flinn commanded. Lola ran over to Riley "I can smell water, lots of it, maybe there is a good place to camp near it?" "Good idea, show me where it is," replied Riley. Lola ran off into the forest, followed closely by Riley. They could hear it before they saw it; a waterfall became visible as they climbed over a large boulder. At is base was a deep pond and Riley could see what looked like the entrance to a cave behind the waterfall. "Let's check that out Lola, behind the waterfall. It might be a good place to camp." They climbed out along a cliff that ran behind the waterfall; it was about six foot up above the surface of the water. The rock was wet and slippery from the spray off the waterfall. As they made their way behind the falling water they found themselves in a large cave, it was well lit from the sun shining through the water. More importantly, it was dry, with enough room for everyone. The pair made their way back to the group and told them what they had found. Flinn told Woody, Hoppy and Colin to go find firewood whilst the rest of them made their way to the cave and set up camp. In the cave there were some large rocks, which they moved around to use as a table and chairs. Woody, Hoppy, and Colin returned with the wood. The rest of them found this hilarious as they tried to get past the waterfall without getting the wood wet; Colin slipping and nearly falling in the pool and screaming like a little girl. They made themselves comfortable whilst Archie set the fire up. "I think I'll have a swim," said Riley walking towards the entrance of the cave. "Ben, you stand guard," said Flinn. Ben got to his feet, grumbling with annoyance. Riley placed his armour down near the entrance. Ben gave him an odd look when he noticed his boxer shorts. He lowered himself down to the water's edge, behind the waterfall, gasping as his feet touched the cold water. Taking a deep breath he let himself drop in, the water stinging his skin with cold. He resurfaced about a metre into the pool and once he had become used to the temperature of the water it was very refreshing. After a few minutes of floating on the surface relaxing he looked over to where Ben had sat, he was no longer there. Looking around he noticed Ben stalking silently towards a large bush about twenty metres away. He then froze and Riley knew, around the bush walked something very big. It was hard to see exactly what it was, but it was definitely the Skerge. Ben was up a nearby tree in the blink of an eye. Riley hid behind a rock at the side of the pond, only visible from the nose up. He looked over at Ben, who was now at the top of the tree. Ben placed a finger to his mouth and told Riley to stay quiet. He then pointed at the cave telling him to get back behind the waterfall. Riley peered around the rock and the Skerge was only a few metres away now, facing the other way. He filled his lungs with air and went under the water. He felt the rock behind him with his feet and pushed off it in the direction of the cave. The pounding of the water was deafening as he swam. He resurfaced at the bottom of the waterfall, gasping for air. Above him all the others were crouched down looking through the falling water, all aware the Skerge was outside. He climbed out shivering and joined them, drying himself on an old rag. "What is it?" Archie asked. "It's a Skerge fighter, but it looks different somehow, "whispered Riley "Different????" Archie queried. "Yes, it moved differently from the Skerge we encountered before," observed Riley. "Is Ben ok?" whispered Ellie." Yes, he is at the top of that big tree," Riley pointed out of the cave, his fingertip getting wet from the falling water.

Ben was sat on a thick branch at the top of the tree. Beneath him, the Skerge fighter walked around the water. He could see that this was no ordinary Skerge. It moved not as if under the control of someone else but as if it was in control of its own actions. He gently climbed down a few branches to get a closer look. He could now see what was different; it looked like no animal he had ever seen. It had no fur just horrible thick skin; its face was disfigured, with a fang at the front of its lower jaw sticking out over its upper lip. He noticed the thing on its neck had become a part of it, the skin had grown around it and it was hardly visible anymore. Its eyes were not the vacant soulless eyes of the previous Skerge. These were burning red and looked alert. It stopped as if thinking about what it had found from looking around the pool. It turned and stared directly at the waterfall, they could not see what it was until it turned to look at them, and now all they could see were those horrible red eyes. They seemed to pierce the water; they all held their breath and stared back. It just stood there staring motionless. Ben knew he had to do something to distract it. He climbed down the back of the tree and ran until the sound of the water was faint. Turning back to where the Skerge was he shouted "Over here! Come on!"

He then headed straight up a nearby tree and waited. He wasn't halfway up the tree and the Skerge was there, looking for whoever had shouted. It didn't stay there long and it ran off again grunting. Ben didn't wait to see if it came back. He ran as fast as he could, back to the cave. Not slowing down he rounded the pool and jumped, flying through the waterfall, narrowly missing everyone's head. He landed near the back of the cave on all fours, his claws out scraping on the floor to slow him down. He stayed there for a second breathing heavily, and gasped "I don't know what that was, but it was a lot more dangerous than any other Skerge." He got to his feet as his breathing became slower. "It seemed it was alive, in control of itself. And it was looking for us, I'm sure of it. the thing on the back of its neck was part of it; it didn't look like it could be removed." They all stood in silence taking it all in. Flinn spoke first "This doesn't change our plan, we need get to the crystal. If we encounter any more of these things then we deal with it." "Deal with it? How do we do that?" asked Archie. "You said that the first Skerge were being controlled as if the animal is still inside and can be saved," quizzed Archie. "Yes! Replied Flinn sternly." "So if these are beyond saving then we have only one option?" Archie pointed out. Nobody spoke, as they all knew what Flinn's next words would be. "We have to kill them!"

They all sat down in silence, "Everyone get some sleep, we will start early again in the morning. I will take first shift keeping guard." Flinn made his way to the entrance of the cave and sat looking through the water. Riley lay on the floor using his armour as a pillow, shivering, he tried to get some sleep. Bear and Lola joined him and curled up either side of him to keep him warm. "Night Dad," Bear said. Riley stroked both Bear and Lola and they all fell asleep.

Riley woke as a cold breeze ran up his back. Lola was no longer lying behind him, but Bear was still curled up in front of him. "Where is Lola?" he asked. "She has gone out to scout the area with Ellie, make sure it's ok outside" Bear said sleepily. Riley got up, put his armour on and climbed out of the cave. The sun was warm and everyone was either drying out their fur or their clothing. Steam was coming off Woody's huge frame as the water evaporated off him. The forest was peaceful and looked beautiful in the morning sunshine. Riley placed his armour down on the floor along with his undergarment; both were wet from the cave. Ruby was sitting on a boulder, legs crossed, face held up into the sun with her eyes closed. Izzy and Archie were at the edge of the pool catching fish, giggling and splashing each other. Woody threw him a big piece of bread, "Breakfast!" he shouted accompanying it with a wink. "Thanks," replied Riley, also with a wink. He stretched out in the sun, chewing on the bread listening to the water; thinking how beautiful it was here. Lola disrupted the peace returning with Ellie, "We can not see or smell any sign of the Skerge sir." Ellie said to Flinn. "Good, everyone pack up your things, we shall continue to the Maze Caves," Flinn advised.

They all dressed and put their armour back on, it felt a lot more comfortable now that it was dry. As they set off again, Bear and Lola were up front, followed by Woody, Hoppy, Izzy and Colin. Riley, Archie, and Ruby were next, and then Ellie and Ben kept watch at the back. All were on high alert at the new danger. "What do you think this new Skerge is?" Archie asked Riley. "I am not sure, I think they may have started out as animals under whatever evil spell, but over time they change into what we saw earlier." "Do you think it is right to kill them?" Ruby quietly said from behind them. "If they really are beyond saving, would you want to be trapped in that nightmare forever?" They both looked at each other but didn't answer.

It was nearly nightfall at the end of the third day of walking when they finally reached the Maze Caves. They waited about a hundred metres away and watched the cave entrance for signs of movement. Night-time was quickly approaching and they needed to make camp for the evening. Next to the cave entrance was a huge oak tree. "We shall sleep on the branches of that tree tonight," Flinn said. The trees branches were thick enough for three of them to sleep side by side, but there were so many they all had one each. Riley found a branch near to the top of the tree. It was curved and acted like a wooden hammock. Leaning over he could see everyone below him chatting quietly and getting comfy in various positions. Ellie climbed up to join him and sat down next to him. They both looked out over the vast forest. "Does your world look like this?" asked Ellie. "Yes, our world is somewhat like yours," replied Riley. He could not tell her that it was nothing like this. "You must be as happy as we were before the Skerge arrived, Things were different then, "said Ellie. He didn't answer, just turned away so Ellie would not see his face and know that he was lying. As he turned he noticed Ruby, she was sitting on the branch next to them. She was staring at Riley, her eyes met Riley's and then she turned to look at the forest, a small smile on her face as if she knew Riley was lying. The sun was setting, casting an orange glow across the treetops, and dark shadows across the forest floor. As the sun fell behind the trees and darkness fell over the forest everyone was quiet, thinking of what might happen tomorrow. The night was quiet and peaceful; Riley watched as one by one everyone fell asleep

 The entrance to the cave was vast. Plants had overgrown the edges and were hanging down from the top. Water dripped down from the roof, it looked very dark inside, "I will not be able to see very well inside the cave, my eyes are not as good as yours, "Ruby said to Flinn. "You're not going in!" said Flinn. "You will stay out here," suggested Flinn, "and Ellie, Ben, and Lola you will go and find the crystal, your eyes are better accustomed to the darkness." He turned to look at Colin "You can go with them; I have heard that you are good at acquiring things that do not belong to you!" Colin thought about arguing but knew he wouldn't win so just walked towards the cave entrance quietly. "Izzy and Archie, you go back up the big tree and be the look out. You will also be safer up there. The rest of us will stay out here; if anything comes we will have to give the others enough time to find the Crystal, "Flinn continued. He looked at Riley, "That means we fight!" Riley gulped. "You will be ok, just stick with us," grinned Woody as he slapped Archie hard on the back, making him stumble forward.

Ellie lit her torch with some flint and then held it down for the others to light theirs on. They headed into the cave; Riley watched as they slowly disappeared into the darkness. The light from their torches took a long time to disappear. Archie and Izzy climbed the tree to take their positions. "Spread out, stay alert and keep quiet," said Flinn. Riley followed Ruby to a large rock near the cave entrance. They both sat on top of it, Ruby looking very vigilant, Riley looking less so. Woody and Hoppy sat at the other side of the cave inside a big bush that covered Hoppy but didn't really cover Woody, his head and beak sticking out of the top. Flinn walked into the woods out of sight. "Where is he going?" asked Riley. "He will keep guard further out into the woods, he likes to be alone," observed Ruby. Bear leaned against the rock beneath Riley and Ruby staring at the spot where Flinn disappeared.

Chapter Nine

The Battle

Ellie could feel the cold air as they walked deeper into the cave. A slight breeze made their torches flicker, their bodies casting huge shadows on the walls. Lola was upfront, smelling the air for any sign of the crystal. "What can you smell Lola?" asked Ben. "Not sure, just damp mainly, there is a strange smell though, very faint. It smells clean like it doesn't belong in here" whispered Lola. "That must be it," said Ellie. They followed Lola deeper and deeper into the cave. They turned left and right many times. "I hope you can find your way out with that nose?"

Ben asked. Lola ignored him and carried on sniffing the air.

Hours seemed to pass slowly; outside the cave they were becoming bored. Hoppy could be heard snoring loudly from the bush, Woody had moved a while ago and was now perched on a branch at the bottom of the big tree. "What's the story with Flinn?" Riley asked Ruby. "Ever since the wolves were hunted to near extinction he has become more and more detached from the rest of us. I can only imagine what it is like being one of the last two left" Ruby replied, thoughtfully. "The Skerge killed all the wolves?" asked Riley. "Why didn't they just take over their minds, like everyone else?" Ruby replied hesitantly "The wolves proved too tough for the Skerge to take over, their minds were too strong and they fought back. So the Skerge killed them to stop the wolves rising up against them." "That's horrible, poor Flinn!" Riley knew now why

Flinn was the way he was. He must have seen some terrible things.

Lola started moving faster; the others had to run to keep up with her. "The smell is getting stronger; the air is cleaner down this way." She turned quickly to the right. A slight blue glow came from the end of a long tunnel. "That is it," shouted Ben. They all ran to the end of the tunnel and it opened up into a large room. Stalactites hung from the ceiling like large fingers grasping for the ground. At the end of the room they could see a stone bath filled with water. A bright blue glow filled the room coming from whatever was in it. They walked over to the bath casually, holding their torches over their head. As they got to the bath they all peered over the edge at once, their faces lit up by the blue glow. At the bottom of the bath was the crystal. It was the size of a large apple and the colour was a beautiful sky blue. "Why is it in water?" asked Colin. "To hide its magic!" answered Ellie. "So when we take it out of the water, what will happen?" asked Colin. "The Skerge will know it's here" Ellie reached in and slowly retrieved the crystal. As soon as it was out of the water the whole room was bathed in a bright blue light. They all stood in silence, waiting for something to happen. But nothing did. After a minute or so Colin said, "Phew I thought something bad was going to happen." A strange scraping noise came from the wall in front of them. Ellie held up the crystal to see what was making the noise. There was a large crack in the wall; the noise was coming from inside. They moved a little closer and the scraping noise stopped. The room suddenly turned very cold, so cold they could see their breath. From the crack in the wall, thick black smoke started seeping out. The smell of the Skerge filled the room making them cough. The smoke became thicker; it seemed to reach out for them like it was alive.

"RUN!" Ellie shouted. Ben, Lola, and Colin ran for the tunnel out of the room. Ellie backed away from the smoke; she placed the crystal in a bag that was tied around her waist. Waving the torch from side to side, she stepped backward slowly. The smoke now reached up to the roof and was spreading out like tentacles towards her. Holding out the torch in front of her, she noticed the smoke winced away from the fire like it was afraid of it. The others were now half way down the tunnel. Knowing she was faster than them, she threw the torch at the middle of the smoke. It moved away from it like a shoal of fish evades a predator, the tentacles of smoke seemingly not wanting the torch to touch them. Ellie ran as fast as her legs would carry her, catching the others before they were at the end of the tunnel. "Lola we need to get out of here fast!" Lola's nose high in the air as she ran, they were running as fast as they could, their torches flickering from the air rushing past.

Outside, the sun started to set behind the canopy of trees. Riley looked around and everyone was visibly nervous. The hair on the back of Bear's neck stood on end, his teeth were showing as he started to growl deeply. They all looked towards the forest, Flinn was walking backward, his sword held out in front of him. A pair of red eyes could be seen in the shadows cast by the setting sun. Then two pairs, then three pairs. Then there were too many eyes to count. Flinn was now level with the rock outside the cave entrance, Bear had joined him, and both were snarling. Riley thought how nasty they both looked. Hoppy came out from his bush, Woody had climbed up to the top of the tree and was now shaking next to Archie and Izzy. Ruby stood up tall on top of the rock and drew her sword. Riley couldn't move with fear, he was transfixed on the eyes staring at them from the darkness. The sun dropped out of sight, leaving the forest in a warm orange glow. The eyes started to move towards them from the darkness. Twelve of the large Skerge fighters walked slowly towards them. All of them looked the same as the one they had encountered at the waterfall, their piercing red eyes flicking between each of them. They lined up next to each other, about twenty metres away and stopped. Riley could just make out their faces, which looked horrible and disfigured. Some had short snouts and some longer. Teeth protruded out of their mouths at all angles. Long sharp claws gripped swords and axes, one had a large bow, with a horribly crooked arrow loaded in it. They were dressed in thick material and leather, stained with dirt and blood. They snarled and barked loudly.

"What are they waiting for?" asked Riley who had joined the rest of them. "We do not have the crystal, that's what they want." Ruby replied, in a surprisingly calm voice. Screams could be heard from inside the cave. They all turned apart from Flinn and Bear who continued snarling at the Skerge. Shadows danced on the walls from the torches in their hands. Ellie was the first to appear from the dark, running so fast she couldn't stop in time. She barged her way past Riley and Ruby, skidding to a stop half way between them and the Skerge. Their red eyes widened as they could see a glimmer of blue light coming from Ellie's bag. Lola, Ben, and Colin appeared soon after, all out of breath. "There is something coming," Ben said gasping for air. He then noticed the Skerge fighters in front of them. "Oh no, what do we do now?" Ellie walked slowly back towards them, covering the bag with her hand. "Whatever are chasing us from the cave are scared of fire. Woody,

Riley, fetch something to burn and block the cave" Ellie shouted. They ran off into the bushes to find some firewood. The largest Skerge fighter was stood in the middle. It raised a big hand and pointed a bony finger towards Ellie. A blood-chilling scream came from its grotesque mouth, making them all shiver. All of them charged at once, the big one going straight for Ellie. Flinn jumped in front of her, swinging his sword, making the Skerge stop and defend itself. "Get that thing out of here" he screamed at Ellie. She used her speed to manoeuvre through the Skerge easily; once she was clear she shot off into the forest so fast she soon couldn't be seen. They were all engaged in the battle now, Flinn fighting off the largest of the Skerge. They were clumsy and slow but immensely powerful. Riley hid behind the large rock, too scared to fight. He watched Bear dance around two of the Skerge, more playing with them than fighting them. Ben was fighting one near to the big tree and Ruby was making fighting two of them look easier than the rest of them. Riley noticed the Skerge that had the bow wasn't joining in with the fight; it was standing at the back drawing its arrow. It released it and the arrow hit Ben in the shoulder with a horrible thud. It sent him flying backward, landing on his back. Bear left the two he was fighting and ran over to where Ben was lying. The Skerge was about to strike Ben with its axe when Bear's sword came out of its chest. It looked down at the sword confused. Bear pulled the sword out and kicked the Skerge in the back. It fell to the floor next to Ben. "Thank you!" Ben said, but Bear was already turning to re-engage the Skerge. Ruby held up her sword to stop both Skerge fighters' swords, she then span fast slicing a deep wound in both their chests. The pair fell, hitting the ground at the same time. Riley looked over at the Skerge with the bow it was now taking aim at Ruby.

He ran at Ruby shouting, "Look out, look out!" Archie could see what was happening, he moved to the edge of the branch, pulled out his dagger and threw it at the archer. It span through the air, hitting the archer just as it released its arrow. Riley ran at Ruby. Watching the arrow all the way, he dived at Ruby, rugby tackling her around the waist. The arrow flew past, narrowly missing Ruby's head. They both landed on the floor in a heap. A Skerge fighter walked over and swung its sword down from over its head towards the pair. Without thinking Riley grabbed Ruby's sword from off the floor, he held it up to stop the oncoming sword; they struck each other, sending sparks flying in all directions. Riley opened his eyes; the Skerge was leaning on its sword pressing down on his. He could smell its breath and drool fell on his chest. Ruby whispered to him "You're starting to remember! "Without thinking, he pushed the sword away; it fell to the floor, sticking in the mud. He jumped to his feet, whilst swinging his sword at the Skerge's forearm. Its hand fell to the floor, still holding its sword. Riley span around the back of it hitting it on the back as hard as he could, it fell forward screaming. Riley froze to the spot thinking about what had just happened. He couldn't believe it, everything was moving in slow motion and slightly blurred. He looked over at Ruby, she smiled at him "Don't think, just let yourself go!" Everything snapped back into focus, as he looked over at Woody, he was dragging a large dead log in one hand and his other arm was full of smaller branches. He was making his way to the entrance of the cave, behind him two Skerge fighters were closing in. He ran over to him, jumping at the Skerge, using the wall next to the cave entrance as a launch point. He brought his sword down on one of the Skerge before it could defend itself. The other punched Riley in the chest, knocking the wind out of him.

Riley fell back against the wall, ducking as the Skerge's sword clanged off the rock face above his head. He used the wall to push himself towards the Skerge, shoulder-barging him away. He cut it across the chest and was off to help Woody before it hit the floor. The battle was raging behind them as they made a fire just inside the entrance. Woody bent down and started to scrape the flint together. Sparks lit up the cave and Riley gasped and fell on his back. Whatever it was that chased Ellie and the others out, was now filling the cave in front of Riley. Its tentacles were reaching out in all directions. "It will not light!" shouted Woody. Colin ran over "Give it to me, you're useless!" He snatched the flint and started to light the fire. The sparks were big enough to make the tentacles move back into the cave. "Got to do this, got to get it lit!" Colin shouted. Woody and Riley stepped backward slowly; mouths open with shock at what they could see in front of them. Colin frantically tried to start the fire; the smoke was almost upon him. With a "whoosh!" the fire started, flames reaching up to the roof of the cave. The tentacles reeled backward in pain, screeching. Colin, Woody, and Riley had to cover their ears. The Skerge left whomever they were fighting with and rushed to the cave entrance. Two of them jumped headfirst into the fire, knocking the burning wood over. Colin, Woody, and Riley had to dive in all directions to dodge the burning wood. The flames subsided and the tentacles moved over the burning Skerge fighters. Colin froze unable to move from fear. Just as the tentacles of smoke got to his face he was barged out of the way. Lola was now standing in the way of the tentacles, "NO!" Riley shouted, scrambling to his feet. Bear who was over by the big tree turned just as the tentacles of smoke hit Lola in the chest. She gasped as if she had jumped into freezing water. More tentacles shot out of the cave, latching on to Lola's legs and arms. It started to envelop her slowly from the legs upwards. Bear ran towards her but was held back by Flinn. Lola turned to Riley, her arm outstretched towards him. As the smoke was just about to cover her face she shouted: "Dad, run!" Riley was frozen to the spot as he watched the smoke cover Lola, her limp body screaming as she was dragged into the darkness of the cave. Riley dropped to his knees in disbelief at what had just happened. With another blood-curdling scream from the cave all the Skerge fighters turned to re-engage them. Flinn ran over and pulled Riley to his feet dragging him away. Woody joined Hoppy, Issy and Archie at the base of the big tree and ran into the forest followed by a few Skerge fighters. "Bear help Ben and follow the others; we will meet you back at the cave behind the waterfall." He picked a large rock up and threw it at one of the Skerge, hitting it on the head. It turned and ran at them, followed by the rest. "Come on Riley, we need to lead them away from the others, now run!" They set off in the opposite direction to the others, closely followed by the Skerge.

Chapter Ten

Reunited

They ran as fast as they could but they could not outrun the Skerge. As they rounded a corner they were confronted by a wide fast-flowing river. Rapids as high as a house smashed against each other, sending huge plumes of mist into the air. It was either fight or take a chance in the river. They both came to the same conclusion and jumped. The water was moving so fast they were tossed around violently. Riley lost sight of Flinn almost immediately as he was thrown around by the strong current. He caught sight of the Skerge watching them get carried away downstream. As he surfaced after being pulled under more times than he could count, he caught a glimpse of the Skerge running off back towards the cave. He turned and his heart sank as he could see the water disappearing over a waterfall. Holding his breath as he went over the edge, his stomach turned as he fell through the air. He seemed to fall for a long time until he finally hit the water at the bottom. The churning water tossed him around like a rag doll, and not knowing up from down he hit the river bed so hard it knocked him unconscious.

He woke slowly, opening his eyes and wincing from the pain in his head. Sitting up blinking in the sunlight, holding his hand up to shade his eyes, he looked around. He was sitting at the edge of the river. It was wide and slow moving, looking almost like a pond. He could see the forest far in the distance. "I must have been floating unconscious for ages". He suddenly remembered Flinn, where was he?. He tried to stand but the pain in his head was too strong. He looked around panicking, downstream and noticed him in the distance lying motionless at the edge of the river. Two hooded figures were walking towards him. He tried to shout but it hurt too much and he couldn't. As the figures got to Flinn they crouched down and started to gently drag him away from the river. Riley tried to shout again but was cut short as someone pulled a blindfold over his eyes from behind him. He tried to struggle but whoever it was, they were extremely strong. They tied his hands and feet and then dragged him backwards. Again he tried to struggle but the pain in his head made him fall unconscious.

He was woken abruptly as he was bounced very hard whilst being dragged along on something. The blindfold had slipped a little, he could make out they were headed uphill as he could see the river far in the distance at the bottom of the valley. After a few hours of being bumped and banged along, the temperature suddenly dropped and he started to shiver. Patches of snow appeared on the ground. Over the next few hours he drifted in and out of consciousness. He was woken suddenly with a large bang as he was dropped on the floor. Three hooded figures were arguing loudly at the entrance to a cave. He was untied from the sledge and carried firmly inside, then thrown to the ground deep inside a cave. The warmth of a fire warmed his face and he could hear voices in the distance. The blindfold was ripped off his face and he was confronted with four hooded figures sitting across from him, two standing and two seated. Behind them another was crouched by the fire warming their hands. "Who are you?" said the largest of them. "Where is Flinn?" he replied. Again he was asked "Who are you?" But this time a lot louder and it was followed by a very deep growl. In a scared voice he replied "My name is Riley, I'm a friend of Flinn's, please tell me where he is and if he is ok", "He is fine, he's resting. He has a very nasty head wound," said a very calm female voice. "How did you end up in the river?" she added. "We were escaping the Skerge, we had recovered the crystal but our party was overrun and we were separated, we jumped over a waterfall to escape." There was silence for a moment then they all took down their hoods to uncover their faces. They were wolves! The female was beautiful looking, a very light grey, almost white. The others looked like they had lived a harder life. The other two that were seated were older and looked very tired; both were a dark brown colour. The two standing were huge, the one who had asked the first question looked battle-hardened and rough. "My name is Lewis" he said. The other was well kept with long, flowing hair which looked a little out of place amongst the squalor of the cave. "And my name is Ethan". The last wolf that was crouching by the fire didn't remove their hood and just stayed by the fire, not moving.

"I thought all the wolves were gone, killed by the Skerge" "So did we" she replied "So imagine our surprise when we come across you and Flinn. We have been hiding here in the mountains for years; it seems the Skerge do not like the cold so we are safe here. We came here when we were hunted, to escape and we thought no one else survived."

"I'm sorry but only Flinn and Fenris are still alive, but the Skerge has him." The wolf by the fire stood quickly and walked towards them. Crouching beside Riley they took off their hood and it was another female, even more beautiful than the first. "Is my father still alive?" she asked "Fenris is your father?" replied a shocked Riley. "Please answer my question." "Yes the council believe he is, they think they need him and the crystal to re-join your world with mine." She stood and walked out of sight into the darkness at the back of the cave. "That's Laurie, Fenris's Daughter and Flinn's sister." That's why Flinn was how he was; he thought his sister had been killed. "Tell us more about the crystal, is it safe?" "Yes I think so. A cheetah named Ellie has it and she ran off into the woods with it. We were supposed to meet up behind the waterfall if we were separated." "Nothing can catch a cheetah, the crystal should be safe," said one of the large wolves who were still standing. "We have to go and make sure all my friends are safe" said Riley. "We will but you need rest and you both need time to heal. Then we will head down the mountain again and help you and your friends" said the first female wolf. "Finally we are getting out of this cave" shouted Ethan, flicking his hair out of his face.

Bear and Ben quickly caught the Skerge that were following the others. They turned to confront them but Bear was on them so fast they had no time to defend themselves. He was mad with rage, swinging his sword around violently. Ben stood and watched in shocked. After the Skerge were dead Bear stopped as if to wake up from his rage. He was covered in blood and breathing heavily. The others joined them and were also shocked at the sight they witnessed. Issy walked over to Bear. "It's ok, we will get her back, she's not lost." Bear just nodded and walked into the forest sobbing.

They followed close behind him but gave him some space. He eventually turned to them. "Flinn said we should head back to the cave behind the waterfall and all regroup there." "You think Ellie got away ok?" asked Issy. "I'm sure she's fine, nothing moves as fast as she does."

Back in the cave Flinn was now awake and was talking to his sister; both had tears in their eyes. Riley smiled as he watched them laugh and smile at each other. "Hi Riley, sorry I didn't introduce myself earlier, I'm Mia." "Nice to meet you," answered Riley still looking at Flinn and smiling. "You're not how I expected humans to be" "What do you mean?" "Well we were brought up to believe you're all evil and only think of yourselves, but you're nothing like that. The way you are looking at Flinn and Laurie it shows me you have a heart." "Thanks, I'm not sure what the humans were like here before but I am nothing like that. I couldn't even lift a sword up until a few days ago." "So why are you here?" "Fenris believes that I can help defeat the Skerge, but I'm not sure." "Well if Fenris believes it then you must be, he's never wrong." "I hope you're right, I really do" Laurie and Flinn appeared from the back of the room. Flinn looked full of life, like nothing had happened to him. Riley couldn't believe his eyes. He was actually smiling. "Thank you Riley" he said "Are you able to move?" Riley got to his feet, a little painfully but he didn't want to show it. "Yes Flinn, ready when you are." "Good everyone gather what you need, we are going to help our friends." "You will be needing this" Mia handed Riley his sword. "We found it a little downstream from where we found you." Everybody collected their things and they all headed down the mountain.

Ben was badly injured and the wound to his shoulder was still bleeding quite badly. "We need to find the cave soon as Ben needs some rest and we need to sort his injured shoulder out" "It is not far now" said Bear "I can smell the river." They got to the cave just as the sun was setting, falling to the floor exhausted. Issy and Archie started to clean Ben's injury. Woody started snoring even before he had sat down properly. "I'll take first watch, you all get some sleep" said Bear. He sat at the edge of the cave looking out through the waterfall for any movement. Everyone was soon asleep. Bear was staring out through the falling water, something moved in the distance. He slowly made his way along the thin ledge towards where the noise was coming from. As he crept into the darkness he stopped in his tracks, "gotcha" said Ellie who had snuck up behind him and was now holding a dagger under his chin. "You make far too much noise Bear" "I knew you were there" "Yeah right sure you did" In the distance they heard a horrible scream, they both looked at each other and ran for the cave. Everyone was still fast asleep; they both stood silently watching for any sign of movement. They could smell the Skerge before they could see them. Three pairs of eyes appeared out of the darkness. A horrible smell of burnt hair hung in the air. One of the Skerge was burnt from jumping on the fire back at the cave. They were slowly searching for them; their eyes were drawn towards the waterfall. Bear gripped his sword tightly, ready to defend the cave. They watched as the Skerge stared right at them, suddenly it flinched as a loud thud could be heard. It fell forward, motionless, into the water, A large arrow was sticking out of its back. Flinn and Laurie ran out from the darkness and started attacking the other two Skerge. The fight was over in a second so as to not make any noise. "I thought there weren't any more wolves left, who is that fighting with Flinn?." "You can come out now, it is safe." They left the cave to join Flinn and Laurie stepping past the burnt Skerge who was still smouldering. "Where did you come from, is Riley with you?" "I'm here, I'm ok" Riley ran towards them with the rest of the wolves. Bear hugged him so hard all the air squeezed out of him. "Where have you been?" "We were rescued by Laurie and the wolves". Laurie nodded her head. The rest of them introduced themselves. Far in the distance the sounds of the Skerge could be heard. "Let's hide these bodies and get inside the cave before more of them turn up." They hid them in a large bush and headed inside.

Laurie woke first to the sound of Woody's snoring; she couldn't believe someone could snore that loudly. "Please shut him up before the Skerge hears him," said Ethan, still lying on the floor with his eyes closed. Laurie crawled over to woody and gently punched him in his massive belly. He woke, startled and confused as he focused on the new wolf in front of him. "What you do that for?" he asked. Ethan sat up "because you were snoring so loudly the whole forest could hear you". Woody looked even more confused as he moved from one new face to the other. Bear and Ellie appeared at the cave entrance. "We have scouted the area and there is no sign of the Skerge."

Ellie said to Flynn, who was now awake, and sat up against the cave wall. "Strange thing though, the bodies are gone!" "No matter, wake the others, we need to get back to the Emerald Valley as soon as we can, the crystal should be safe there."

A short time later they were all awake and heading out of the cave. "Ethan, Lewis, you go back and get the elders and meet us at the bramble wall' said Flinn. They both ran off into the forest.

They headed off with Flinn, upfront along with Bear; he was sniffing the air as usual to make sure the coast was clear. Woody was at the back chewing on his breakfast whilst Hoppy nervously scanned the forest for danger. The forest was strangely quiet as they passed through it. Not a sound could be heard until Bear shouted, "Stop" and held up his hand. Everyone drew their weapons and waited. "I can smell them, lots of them, in all directions, getting closer." They all started scanning the forest with panicked looks. "How far away is the bramble wall?" Riley asked. "It's not far now". He paused to consider what to do next, "RUN!" Bear shouted before Flinn could carry on. They all ran as fast as they could, Ellie was out of sight within seconds; they caught up with her at the bramble wall. "I don't understand" said Bear "I can smell them everywhere but can't see anything." He was sniffing the air frantically, until he suddenly stopped, staring deep into the forest, growling. "Oh no that's not good," said Archie gulping loudly. They could see movement; Ethan, Lewis and the elders were running so fast they were tripping over themselves. "GO" Ethan shouted "they are right behind us." The forest started to grow dark, in the distance Skerge fighters could be seen walking slowly towards them, in their hundreds. In the middle were around thirty of the larger ones, easily noticeable with their blazing red eyes.

They stopped around a hundred meters away, thick smoke rising from the middle. They parted and the smoke rolled out in front of the line of fighters, horrible tentacles reaching out in all directions. Ethan and the others collapsed when they got to them, "they have been chasing us ever since we came down the mountain." His words hardly recognisable due to him gasping for breath.

It was eerily quiet and nothing moved. "Ellie, Ben!" shouted Flinn. "Get them through the wall, NOW!" They both began to frantically chop their way through, the rest following closely behind. Flinn and Ruby drew their swords just as arrows began to rain down on them. Riley moved next to them and together they tried to deflect the arrows. Riley managed to hit a few and dodge the rest; Flinn and Ruby swatting them out of the sky with ease. Slowly they backed into the path cut into the wall, arrows thudded into the wall all around them. It snapped shut in front of them, they could hear the arrows hitting still the brambles. On the other side they all stood staring at the wall, listening to the Skerge try to break through. "Can they get through?" asked Riley, out of breath. "Only magic can breach the wall and they have none, so we are safe" replied Ruby reassuringly.

Chapter Eleven

The Skerge revealed

They headed to the village, Riley thinking again how beautiful the valley was. As they walked through animals came out to meet them, asking questions about what had happened. Nobody replied they all just made their way to the big house to tell the rest of the council. Flinn and Ruby went in whilst the rest of them waited outside on the steps. They were all worn out; quietly they waited to see what the council would say. Villages began to gather at the bottom of the steps, angry that they did not know what was happening. After about an hour Ruby came out of the large door, followed by the rest of the council. "The Skerge are at the wall. Don't worry, they cannot enter the valley, we are quite safe." The entire village had now gathered and were all listening intently to what Ruby had to say. Riley noticed how none of them seemed scared. Ruby was well-respected, everyone trusted her. "We need to know where they have Fenris; we are devising a plan to retrieve him. We have stationed guards at various points along the wall, if anything happens they will let us know. Please stay calm we will let you know if anything else happens." The crowd slowly dispersed with mixed emotions. "I'm off for some food and a lie down" said Woody as he headed off to the inn. Riley, Bear, Ben and Ellie stayed on the steps as Ruby joined them. "Ben go and see the healers and make sure your shoulder is healing ok." "Yes ma'am." he replied. You three come in the house we need to think of a plan." They followed Ruby into the big house, "we need to look in Fenris's Study to see if there is any information on the Skerge".

The staircase was wide enough for the three of them to fit side by side, the wood was carved with the same ornate patterns as the front door. They made their way up to the third floor, the door to Fenris's Room was open; Laurie sat at a desk looking through old pieces of paper. "Found anything of interest?" asked Ruby. "No nothing that could help, just a load of gibberish really."

A badger came bursting into the room out of breath, "Something has come through the wall ma'am." "What has?" "We don't know ma'am, the bramble wall just parted and something walked through. It is wearing a cloak and hood and is just standing there, not moving. Flinn has taken some troops to see what it is." "Thank you." The badger then left in a hurry. "Ellie catch them up and see what it is" she left the room so fast the paper on the desk flew in the air.

Riley made his way over to a huge bookshelf on the far wall; most of them were in a language he had never seen before. "What language are these books written in?" he asked. Without looking up from the pile of paper in front her Laurie said "its old wolfish, an ancient language the wolves used to speak." Riley carried on looking at the books. On the top shelf almost hidden between two larger books was a small notebook. He could see that the dust had not settled on it as much as the others. He reached up and got it down. It looked old; all the edges were ripped and discoloured. Inside it was a mess, scribbles and doodles covered every page. "Can anyone read wolfish?" he asked, "Yes I can" replied Laurie again not looking up from the desk. "This looks like it has been used more than the other books." Riley handed her the book. As she started to read, her expression slowly began to look upset, until she started to cry. "What's wrong?" Ruby said putting her hand on Laurie's shoulder. "It starts off with ways he thought to defeat the Skerge, but then it all starts to get really angry. He just repeats the same things over and over again. 'humans DIE' and 'merge the worlds'. What does he mean?" Nobody spoke, Ruby looked visibly shocked. Laurie turned the pages and the same thing was written over and over again. In the middle of the book she found an old piece of cloth folded up; the writing was faded and hard to make out. She placed it on the table. "Its old magic, very dark". She paused and a horrified look fell across her face. "Oh no!" She looked at Ruby "the only other person that could come through the wall like that is….." she stopped talking and they both ran out of the room. Riley tried to keep up but they left him far behind, he lost sight of them and didn't catch them up again until he reached the wall. Flinn was approaching the hooded figure. It was a little taller than Flinn, its dark cloak was ripped and filthy from being dragged on the floor behind it. Whoever it was did not speak and was standing motionless. Flinn gripped his sword cautiously, walking slowly "Who are you and what do you want?" he asked. The hooded figure did not answer, its cloak moving slightly in the breeze. "Flinn stop!" shouted Laurie, "Its …. " She did not have time to finish as the figure reached up and pulled the hood off slowly, revealing its face. "NO!" Flinn said in shock. Loud gasps came from everyone watching. "Yes son it is me" said Fenris, looking very old and tired. Flinn stumbled back a few steps with the shock. "It can't be you. All the pain and suffering. WHY?!" his voice rose with anger. "Surely you know why son, everything the humans did to us, I want to take it back. We need to merge the worlds again and take back the land the humans stole from us." With a quiet and horse voice he seemed to struggle getting his words out as if his throat had not seen any water in weeks. "This is madness, you have turned the animals into monsters and now you want to start a war with the humans." The anger in Flinn's face was scary. Laurie walked up behind Flinn and gently put her hand on his shoulder. Flinn jumped and the anger seemed to fade from his face. "I want you both to join me, become one of my minions and we will become unstoppable." He reached out one of his hands. It was withered and shaking slightly. "Never" shouted Flinn, slapping Fenris's outstretched hand. He staggered backwards, holding his hand to his chest in pain. His face turned nasty and his eyes turned blood red, thick black smoke started to form at his feet. Behind him the bramble wall shook and trembled. It slowly opened as if it was being forced to do so. Hundreds of pairs of red eyes could be seen staring back at them through the gap in the wall. As the smoke around Fenris grew and became thicker, something started to walk through the wall towards them. "Lola!" Riley and Bear Shouted at the same time. She was walking slowly without any emotion or reaction to Riley and Bear. She looked filthy; her armour was bedraggled and ill-fitted. Her ears were swept back and her eyes were glazed over with pain and sadness. She was about halfway through the wall when the other Skerge fighters started to make their way through. Some animals began to panic and run but most stayed and drew their weapons. Ellie reached inside her bag and pulled out the crystal. The bright sunlight in the valley hit it and flashes of brilliant blue light shone out in all directions. She held it high in the air and ran at Fenris. Flinn and Laurie covered their eyes as she ran past. Fenris screamed loudly as if in immense pain. Ellie stopped and held the crystal out in front of her. A bright blue beam of light shone straight at Fenris. The smoke that surrounded him seemed to be blown backwards as if it were caught in a strong wind. Lola and the other Skerge ran back out of the wall. Fenris was now standing as if he was caught in a strong wind. He was fighting against the light and wind, struggling to stay where he was. With one last attempt he tried to walk forwards but the wind was now too strong and with a loud "NOOOOO" he was blown backwards through the gap in the wall, the brambles snapping shut with force.

Ellie placed the crystal back in her bag and the bright light faded. Everyone was looking at her, blinking, and rubbing their eyes in amazement. "Wow, how did you know to do that?" asked Archie excitedly. "I'm not sure; it was like I just knew it would work, I also know that he will not be coming back through. Whatever magic he used to open the brambles has gone, for how long I do not know."

Fenris screamed at the wall with anger. The other Skerge cowered around him. Raising his hand, he gestured at the brambles to move but nothing happened. Again he let out a horrifying scream. He reached out and grabbed a deer by the neck that was standing too close. The deer struggled, then passed out, falling to the floor . He turned to Lola "you will be my weapon, first I need to regain my strength." She walked towards him as smoke began to appear around them both. The smoke carried them off into the forest as if it was being blown by a breeze.

Riley followed the rest of them back to the village. He couldn't get the sight of Lola out of his head. She looked horrible, in so much pain. What if they couldn't save her in time and she was lost in the nightmare. "Don't worry dad" said Bear who had joined him without Riley noticing. "We will rescue Lola." Riley just nodded and stayed quiet as he did not share Bear's enthusiasm.

Back at the big house they all sat at the table. "Firstly, is there anything else we need to know about the crystal Ellie?" asked Flinn "I am not sure, I do not know why I knew that the crystal would do what it did. I think it made me do it, I cannot explain it. I also know that Fenris has drained his magic and needs to regain it, and for that he needs darkness. He needs to go back to the place he found the dark magic." "Ok, it sounds like Fenris is weak so we should attack now." Flinn seemed to come alive whilst he was speaking. "If you need to re-arm go and do so. If not, I suggest you get some food and rest, tomorrow we find his lair and destroy him." He turned and disappeared into the back of the house. Ruby addressed the room "I suggest everyone do as Flinn says, make sure you're all rested. Laurie maybe there is something we have missed up stairs?

Riley felt lost in his own thoughts. maybe if he had some food he would feel better, so he headed to the inn. When he got there Woody was already stuffing his face whilst Hoppy sat next to him nibbling on a carrot. He sat down across from them and was joined by Bear and Ben. "How is it?" he asked looking at the mix of leaves and mud covering Ben's shoulder. "Not bad actually, the healers here are amazing. I should be nearly fixed by morning." They all settled down to eat in silence.

A large cave lay deep in the woods, it was quiet and peaceful. The breeze gently moved the surrounding trees from side to side. The peace was suddenly broken by the sound of a howling wind, the noise you would hear as a tornado approached. The branches of the trees were now moving more violently, sounds of wood splintering and snapping filled the forest. Thick black smoke spiralled in the wind as it moved quickly through the forest towards the cave. It stopped close to the entrance; the wind began to slow. As the smoke settled Fenris and Lola emerged from the smoke as it started to disappear. Fenris walked towards the cave entrance, Lola stood motionless. He raised a shaking hand and muttered some words under his breath. A few seconds past and the rock that surrounded the cave entrance began to change. Grey became deep black, cracks started to appear accompanied by horrible sounds of rocks in pain. Thick black liquid oozed from the cracks like blood from an open wound. Fenris began to walk inside, followed by a zombified looking Lola. Large rotten wooden cages with around twenty animals in each were lined up next to the entrance of the cave entrance, a Skerge guard stood next to the door to each of them. One of the bigger Skerge, a horribly disfigured rat walked towards the first cage and opened the door; the occupants started to scream and scrambled towards the back of the cage. An old fat badger was grabbed roughly by the scruff of its neck and dragged kicking and screaming out of the cage. The guard slammed the door shut its red eyes staring at the animals still whimpering in the corner. The rat dragged the badger deep inside the cave followed by Fenris; screams could be heard deep in darkness. The badger pleaded with the rat to let him go, the rat did not listen or even acknowledge him. They came to a large room; it was dimly lit with a few candles flickering on the walls. Fenris stood by entrance to the room with a horrible grin across his face; he was enjoying watching the badger in pain. The badger was thrown to the floor, he sat still too scared to move, he looked around the room and red eyes looked back at him. His eyes started to adjust to the low light and he could make out a strange looking tree stump in the far corner of the room, it was big and rotten with a hole at the base of it. A strange humming sound was coming from deep inside. The badgers face turned to horror as the humming noise became louder; he could see what was making it. A small bug crawled slowly out of the hole, it was covered in a thick black liquid. The liquid dripped off of its back as it walked leaving a trail behind it. The badger was frozen with fear as the bug moved closer. One of the guards grabbed him holding him down as the bug crawled up the badgers arm; its legs scratching him making him wince with pain. The bug stopped at the badger's neck; with a loud screeching noise it buried its legs into the badger's skin. The badger screamed with pain but then fell silent, its eyes glazed over and a vacant expression fell across its face. The guard loosened its grasp as the badger got to its feet and then silently made its way out of the cave as if in a trance. Inside was dark; flickers of light came from lava seeping from the walls. Thick choking smoke billowed from the cracks left by the lava; it clung to the roof moving as if alive. Deeper into the cave they walked, the occasional scream could be heard from somewhere in the cave. Fenris gave a wry smile after he heard each one. They entered a large room; a river of lava ran through the middle of it casting shadows across the jagged walls. A bridge crossed the river and on the other side was a huge throne carved out of the rock and decorated with bones and jewels. Fenris sat slowly with a long drawn out groan. He lifted his finger, and two huge black bears stumbled out of the shadows either side of the throne, taking up guard positions in front of Fenris. Lola moved to his side, still without any emotion. "I need rest" he barked "I will be weak now, so you will be my protection." He pulled his hood over his head so all that was visible were his red eyes. Slowly they began to fade to black.

Riley jumped as there was a loud knock at his bedroom door. "Ten minutes, outside!" said a voice he didn't recognise. Sitting up in bed, he rubbed his eyes, he must have fallen asleep without knowing it as he was still wearing his armour. Picking up his sword from next to his bed he made his way downstairs. Woody came out of his room just in front of him, he was so large he nearly couldn't fit down the corridor. In the bar area everyone was finishing up food or getting their things ready to go outside. Woody started ramming food in his mouth that had been left, at the same time stuffing food in to his bag for later. Riley picked up some fruit, bread and a flask of water and joined the rest of them outside. He was stopped in his tracks by at least forty soldiers made up of different animals, all lined up in full armour. Huge spears reached up in to the sky as they stood to attention. Flinn was standing at the front facing them, looking very proud. The quiet was soon broken though as Woody struggled to get out of the door behind Riley, His huge frame almost getting stuck in the door. "Sthnorry" he said with his mouth full of food. Archie and Issy sniggered as Woody made his way to the back of the group, closely watched by Flinn with an angry gaze. Riley followed him and was waved over by Bear and Ellie who were wearing their newly cleaned armour, shining in the morning sun. Bear handed Riley one of two round shields he was holding. They looked like steel, but felt as light as a feather each with ornate gold trim. "The blacksmith has made us these; he said they were strong enough to stop an axe blow from a wild forest bear!" The soldiers all started banging their spears on the floor in unison. First slowly and then gradually faster until they all stopped at the same time. Flinn began to walk backwards and forwards, holding his sword down by his side. "Now we march against the Skerge, we must defeat this evil before our world is lost forever. You are all aware that my father is behind this madness; if any of you get the chance do not hesitate, strike him down, do not show him any mercy. You are our last hope, we must not fail." He turned to face towards the bramble wall and held his sword high in the air, light reflected off its blade and danced across the many faces of the soldiers "Follow me my brothers and sisters, follow me into the darkness." and with that he let out an almighty howl. A chorus of roars, squawks and growls filled the air. Riley had to cover his ears it was so loud. Flinn headed towards the wall and the soldiers followed in perfect formation. A chill ran down Riley's spine as he thought of what was to come. His face must have given away the fear he was feeling. "Don't worry Riley, all will work out in the end" said Ruby, placing a reassuring hand on his shoulder. She smiled and set off towards the wall. Riley took a deep breath and tried to muster some courage. The air was then swiftly knocked out of him as Woody gave him an almighty slap on the back. "Come on lad, let's go and sort this stupid old wolf out." He swung his huge axe on to his shoulder and they both set off towards the wall. No one spoke as they followed the battalion of soldiers up the hill towards the wall. The noise of them marching was almost deafening, Riley looked around and everyone had scared and apprehensive faces. Except Woody, who was sauntering along as if on an afternoon walk in the park. He wished he could be as relaxed as Woody was. Inside he was petrified but he did not want to show the others so he walked tall and proud. He turned to look at Ruby who as always looked graceful in her finest armour. She gave him a reassuring smile and turned back towards the soldiers. Before long they had reached the bramble wall, it was quiet and peaceful. Riley thought how beautiful it was and wished the impending battle did not wait on the other side of the wall. Laurie made her way through the soldiers who moved around her like fish would around a shark. She stopped about a meter from the brambles and opened the book they found in Fenris's study. As she muttered some words under her breath the bramble began to shake. "Present arms" shouted Flinn and the soldiers held their shields up to form a wall with their swords ready to strike if anything came through the wall. Woody, Ruby and the others all stood ready, eyes transfixed on the ever-widening gap in the bramble wall. Riley tried to look brave even though he was petrified at what was about to come charging towards them. The brambles were now wide open and nothing had come through, they couldn't see anything at the other side. Nothing moved and there was an eerie silence. "Ellie, Ben, go and scout ahead and see what's out there" barked Flinn. They both ran off into the forest and were out of sight in seconds. The soldiers stayed in tight formation just in case it was a trap. After a few minutes Woody puffed out his cheeks, swung his huge axe onto his shoulder and headed though the wall. Murmurs of confusion came from the soldiers but were cut off with a loud growl from Flinn. "Come on Riley" said Ruby, waving her hand after Woody. Riley jogged towards her and they both followed the huge Bird into the forest. "Wait there" shouted Flinn as he walked towards them. They stopped at the edge of the forest; Archie, Issy and Colin had now joined them. Ellie came speeding back through the forest towards them. She skidded to a stop next to them. "Nothing Sir" she said slightly out of breath. "Nothing at all." Ben came back through the canopies of the trees and landed silently in front of them. "They all left sir, all of them in the same direction. The tracks all head the same way." He pointed deep into the forest. It was the middle of the day but far away in the distance it was as black as night, the distant rumble of thunder could be heard from where Ben had pointed. "That is where they have all gone," said Laurie. "Back to the place Fenris became the Skerge. He must be weak now and all his army will be there to protect him." "That is where we will go," growled Flinn, and he turned and walked back toward the soldiers. Riley couldn't make out what he was saying. He was pointing at individual soldiers and each in turn walked out of the formation and lined up in front of him. They looked mean and war-hardened; a huge stag with armoured antlers and a petite female otter that had two swords crossed across its back. They all headed back towards them as the bramble wall slowly closed, sealing the rest of the soldiers in the Emerald Valley. "I have brought the best soldiers in my army to join us; the rest will be left to defend the valley if we fail" said Flinn in a stern voice. This didn't make Riley feel any better about what was about to come. They all set off into the forest towards the darkness and thunder rumbling in the distance. Occasional flashes of lightning made Riley jump, he hoped it had gone unnoticed until Ellie and Bear came over to walk beside him. "You ok Riley?" asked Ellie "It's only a bit of lightening" "It's not the lightening I'm worried about." Riley answered, trying not to sound to scared. "If we get there before Fenris is healed then we will have a good chance of stopping him. The way you dealt with the Skerge last time you'll be ok," said Bear, waving his sword in the air and pretending to fight. Riley didn't answer as he noticed Ben ahead standing still with his hand in the air. "Quick hide" he said as he shot up a nearby tree with ease.

Everyone scattered in all directions and were hidden before Riley could even think about moving. "Psssst, here, quick," Bear's hand was waving him over to a large bush to his right. He ran over and was dragged in. Everyone was quiet, waiting to see what was coming. Riley shivered as the temperature dropped suddenly; his nostrils were filled with the horrible smell of decay. Two pairs of red eyes emerged slowly out of the dark shadow cast by a large tree near to the one Ben was hiding in.

Chapter Twelve

"Shoot the walls"

A small goat limped out of the shadows dragging a spear behind it. Its face was blank, showing no sign of emotion. There was a large cut on its shoulder that was half healed; blood seeped from it down its arm. The second pair of eyes stayed longer in the shadows before walking slowly into the light. It was one of the bigger Skerge fighters; its head swept side-to-side scanning the forest. It was a huge hare, with its ears bound tightly behind its head and down its back. It moved with a purpose unlike the goat, which stumbled about in a daze. The hare pushed the goat out of its way as it moved forward towards them. Riley could see

Ben moving in the trees above the goat, he perched just above it, his dagger held sideways in his mouth. He dropped silently to the ground, and taking the dagger out of his mouth he crept up behind the goat, then with a quiet flick of his wrist he cut the parasite off the goat's neck and it let out a horrible scream. The hare turned sharply to see what was making the noise, and before it had time to react Ellie ran past so fast she was nearly a blur. She cut the hare across its neck; it stopped not knowing it was injured, trying to scream but couldn't as its throat was cut. Falling to its knees, it made a horrible gurgling noise and then fell forward dead. Ellie came speeding back in and skidded to stop next to the hare, "These must have been scouts, sent to find us, there will be more than just these two". A loud screech came from deeper in the forest "They must have heard the goat scream" said Ellie, readying herself for what was on its way. Three huge bears came crashing through the forest towards them, they were horribly disfigured; their fur was filthy and matted with blood. Out of nowhere, the otter back-flipped towards the bears, and just as they lunged for her she leapt high in the air pulling both swords from behind her back. She brought the swords down across the middle of the bear's chest sending it screaming in pain backwards. The other two screamed and charged at her but she cartwheeled away acrobatically. The stag thundered out of its hiding place, its nostrils flared with its head down, he rammed one of the bears in its side sending it flying through the air and slamming into a tree, almost knocking it to the floor. The last bear was confused whom to attack and as it started to run at the stag there were two loud thuds. The bear staggered around flailing its arms until it fell forward hitting the ground, sending dust into the air. Ruby stood in the distance holding her bow out in front of her; she had hit the bear with two arrows in its back. Everyone stood silent, ready for the next attack. After a minute or so nothing came so they put their weapons away. Riley, Bear and the others joined the rest of them next to the slain Skerge fighters. "Wow, you two are amazing", said Bear to the otter and the stag. "Thank you, my name is Kate and this is Troy" The stag strode over to them, towering over Bear and Riley. "Pleased to meet you" he said in a deep gravelly voice. Flinn was inspecting the body of the hare "I knew him, he was an old friend, he went missing some time ago." He knelt down beside the hare and closed his eyes. "The Skerge must know we are on our way now after that, everyone stay alert from here on in, any noise call it out, do not attack alone, and stay quiet". He stood and turned to face them all "When we get to the Skerge lair we will be outnumbered, form a circle back to back and fight outwards, do not get separated, as soon as we defeat Fenris his army should fall." He started walking towards the darkness once again. Riley held his sword and shield tightly and hoped he would be able to do what he did last time he was in danger. He had to stop doubting himself and believe. He knew that soon enough he would find out. Darkness started to surround them, the air turned colder; and Riley could see his and everyone else's breath. The strong stench of decay hung in the air again. "We must be getting close" whispered Ben. Riley held his shield a little higher and crept slowly forward. Out of the blackness bright red eyes started to appear, at first only a few then quite soon they were surrounded. "Everyone form a circle around Laurie" barked Flinn. "Ellie give Laurie the crystal, if we can't use it to defeat Fenris then destroy it." They stood shoulder to shoulder waiting for the battle to begin. "Come on!" shouted Bear at the eyes staring at them. Ruby had joined Laurie in the middle of the circle, her bow ready to fire at the first thing to attack. Nothing moved and there was a terrifying silence. From out in the darkness there was a scream so loud it made them all cover their ears. It started to get lighter and easier to see. A cave could be seen through the easing blackness. The smell of oil was thick and almost choking; it dripped from the walls and flowed slowly into cracks in the ground at the base of the cave. Two red eyes moved slowly towards them from inside the cave. Thick black smoke slithered out of the entrance, Fenris emerged gliding on the smoke. His thick black cloak dragged on the floor behind him; his hood was up covering his face. He edged his way out of the cave and stopped motionless.

"Drop your weapons," said Fenris in a quiet and crackled voice, "I said DROP THEM!!!!!!" his voice boomed loudly, the smoke that swirled around him shot out in all directions as if it had been electrocuted. Everyone slowly lowered their weapons. "Have you come to destroy me, your own father?"

"You are not my father anymore" replied Flinn with disdain. "And what of my daughter, does she share your views?" He pulled his hood back as he was asking the question. Laurie gasped at the sight of his face; she did not answer but covered her eyes with her hands and sobbed. Fenris was barely recognisable anymore. His face was so gaunt his cheekbones were visible under his thin grey skin. The fur had all but gone from his head, his ears were curled and his teeth were a dark yellow. He stretched out a bony hand "give me the crystal and I might let you live." Ellie put her hand on the bag "Do not let him have the crystal" said Flinn "if they try and take it run, and don't stop." "You cannot escape my Skerge fighters; there is no way out for you now." Fenris laughed at them but it soon changed into a horrible rattling cough. Ellie held her bag close to her chest, winked at Riley and flashed past the Skerge before any of them could move. Fenris slowly lowered his hand "get them" he muttered. The Skerge all charged at once, Riley picked up his sword and shield just as a large wart hog jumped at him. He span quickly to the left, missing the hog by inches, it tripped trying to turn to get him. Riley followed it to the floor with his sword. He closed his eyes and could feel the blade as it hit the hog on its back; with a loud squeal it was dead. He looked up; he wasn't scared anymore. He knew if he just trusted his instincts he'd be ok. The battle was ferocious; Ruby was firing arrows with surgical accuracy, Skerge fighters dropped all around as she fired arrow after arrow with unbelievable speed. Archie, Issy and Colin worked as a team darting quickly from left to right, confusing the slow moving Skerge. Flinn was striking them down with ease, with every thrust of his sword another Skerge fighter fell to the ground. Riley was horrified to see Bear violently swinging his sword left and right as he walked a direct path towards Fenris. He was mad with rage shouting "where is she you monster, where is my sister?" Riley dodged an axe swinging at his head and ran as fast as he could towards Bear. He tackled him to the floor, "no Bear stop, what you are doing?" Two Skerge fighters swung their axes down towards Riley and Bear. The floor rumbled underneath them as Boris hit the Skerge with all his might, sending them flying up in the air. "ENOUGH!" shouted Fenris holding his arms in the air. Thick black smoke began to appear all around them, blinding them. Riley couldn't breathe, he could hear the others struggling for breath in the darkness. He was suddenly grabbed from behind by something big and immensely powerful. A huge bear held him so tightly he dropped his weapons and couldn't move. Twinned with the smoke he felt himself slipping into unconsciousness. The smoke started to clear and whatever had hold of him loosened its grip. He could see that the same fate had become the rest of them, each being held from behind. Troy had three holding him on the floor, and they were struggling at that. "That's enough of that," said Fenris walking towards them, "tut, tut, tut," shaking his bony finger at them all. He turned towards the cave entrance, Lola appeared looking horrifying, her fur was filthy and matted; she looked as if she hadn't eaten or slept in days. There was a vacant expression on her face and she swayed hauntingly. "Come my dear, come to your master." She shuffled towards Fenris as if drunk, stopping in front of him. He turned to look at Bear with a horrible smile on his face, "Now let me start again, give me the crystal or she dies." "NO!" he groaned in agony as the Bull that was holding him squeezed tighter. "I'll ask once more, give it to me, or, SHE DIES!" He sounded furious, placing a knife to Lola's throat. Bear struggled in desperation as Fenris applied pressure; a small trickle of blood began to seep from a cut on Lola's neck. Riley could not see any other way out "Ellie if you are out there bring the crystal back, please" There was no reply; Riley started to panic as Bear howled loudly. Fenris growled deeply "ok I gave you a chance, now your friend dies" he hung on his last word as if he enjoyed saying it. He pulled the knife back then stopped, staring at something in the sky. There was a strange whistling sound, as if something was falling towards them. With a loud thud a flaming arrow landed at the feet of Fenris. He instantly reeled backwards in pain. Another two arrows followed, hitting the ground just in front of Fenris.

Then Riley knew what to do "Ellie, shoot the walls around the cave," he realised the thick black liquid was oil. There was another loud whistling sound; Riley caught sight of the arrow high in the air. It passed straight over his head as if in slow motion it landed perfectly in the oil. With a bang, it went up in flames. The front of the cave burned wildly, Fenris was flailing his arms around in pain. The Skerge fighters that were holding them released their grip. The Skerge that had the parasites on their necks fell to the floor writhing around. The others were doing as Fenris did, staggering in pain. The flames caught the back of Fenris's cloak, and he was engulfed in flames. The Skerge fighters also caught fire without being near any flames. The Skerge on the floor lay motionless; the flames did not affect them. Ellie came running in to join them as they watched the madness before them. Fenris struggled to get his cloak off to escape the flames. He screamed as he walked towards them, his body was almost skeletal without his cloak to cover him. His fur was burnt from the fire, his eyes burned brighter than the flames behind him. "Give me the crystal" struggling to get his word out.

"It must be destroyed" Ellie spoke quietly as if in a trance. "He will never stop unless the crystal is destroyed." She reached in her bag and retrieved the crystal. Fenris seemed to come alive again and ran towards them "NOOOOOO" he screamed. Flinn grabbed the crystal and threw it to the ground; he brought his sword down hard on the crystal. Time seemed to stand still as the crystal shattered into a thousand pieces. A shock wave emanated from the broken crystal knocking everyone off their feet, it also blew the fires out as it passed over them. A shaft of light shone through the dark clouds and reflected off the shards of the crystal, a million tiny shafts of light shone in all directions. The Skerge slowly started to turn to smoke, disappearing as if caught in a light breeze. Fenris also slowly turned to smoke, starting from his feet upwards, he was being blown away. As he was disappearing his eyes slowly lost their redness, his face turned back to the way it was before the Skerge. "I am sorry my son," Fenris spoke in his old clear voice "please forgive me?" Flinn held out his hand longingly "Father" as the last of Fenris disappeared. Everyone stood in silence not knowing what to say. The silence was broken by the noises of coughing and spluttering, the parasites on the necks of the Skerge started to drop off now that Fenris was no longer in control of them. They were now slowly dying on the floor next to their former hosts. The animals were slowly turning back to their old selves again. Riley and Bear both shouted at once "LOLA!" they ran towards her lying on the floor, she lay still next to Fenris's burnt cloak, with a jolt she sat upright gasping for air. "You're alive" cried Riley, hugging Lola and Bear.

The animals all awoke from their nightmare, dazed and confused. Riley looked around and reflected on what had just happened in amazement.

It felt like only a short walk back to the bramble wall, explaining to the rescued animals on what they'd gone through.

Flinn held both hands up to the wall and muttered some words, the wall moved differently this time. It retracted back into the floor and disappeared beneath the lush green grass.

All the soldiers were standing guard, A few seconds passed, then they opened into rapturous applause at the sight of them returning safely.

The great hall was full; animals spilled out into the surrounding forest. Celebrations and parties were in full swing. As Riley approached the crowd they are all turned and cheered. It was so loud it shocked him and stopped him in his tracks. Bear and Lola on the other hand soaked it all in like a pair of teenage pop stars. Ruby placed her hand on Riley's shoulder "Come on Riley, after all we have been through don't let this stop you." They walked into the great hall to more cheering; Flinn was standing proud at the back of the hall waving them over. The council were all lined up behind him along with Archie, Ellie and the rest. With a loud roar from a lion the hall fell silent. "We are gathered here today to say thanks to the brave few that saved us from the nightmare that was the Skerge" boomed the lion. "I now hand you over to the great black wolf" The hall erupted once more as Flinn stepped forward. "Thank you my friends, we are now free from the nightmare of the Skerge." The room erupted again, "I would like to present the small group of heroes with the 'Animals Against Adversary' medal for their bravery." He called out each of them in turn, placing the medal around their neck. "And finally, he is now the first human to receive this medal, He is now a friend to us all, Riley". Riley stepped forward "You are now a part of a very special group of animals, and you are my friend." Riley held his medal in the air as the hall cheered loudly. Flinn held his hand up and the hall slowly fell quiet again. "We must now send Riley back to the human world." He pointed at the mirror that Riley first came through. "Can I come back and see you all again?" "Yes of course, the gateway will always be open for you and Bear." Riley turned to look at Lola, "Lola, are you staying here?" "Yes Riley, Flinn asked me to stay. I hope you understand." "Yes of course I understand if that is what you want." He turned to Flinn and shook his hand "Please take care of her." "I give you my word," replied Flinn. Riley made his way over to the mirror as Bear hugged Lola goodbye.

Flinn called Riley back before he could go through the mirror. "I want to give you a parting gift before you go." He placed his hand on Bear's shoulder muttering a few words under his breath. Riley wondered what Flinn was doing but didn't ask. Bear went through the mirror first, closely followed by Riley.

The Forest was quiet; shafts of light broke through the tree canopy. Bear ran out from the bottom of the tree and out into the forest. Riley soon followed blinking in the sunlight. "Bear, Bear where are you?"
"I'm coming"
Bear ran up to Riley wagging his tail. "I can still understand you" said Riley as Bear jumped up at him excitedly. "This is brilliant" shouted Bear, running around in circles.

They both walked back home through the forest towards the lake, playing out their adventures, Bear stopped and growled as they approached the lake, Tommy Banks and his mates were sitting by the water's edge. "It's ok Bear, calm down"

"You want me to take care of them?" said Bear still growling

Tommy stood up grabbing a big branch as he did. "Talking to your stupid dog now are you, mummy's boy?"

"And whose fancy dress party is it? Ha-ha and even his stupid dog is dressed up" said one of the other boys, making the others laugh. Riley hadn't realised he was still wearing his armour. Bear had now stopped growling and sat down. "So Bear would you like to deal with this?"

"Actually Riley, after you." Bear said, leaning on a nearby tree.

Riley drew his sword with a smile "Ok Tommy, give me your best shot."

The End

Printed in Great Britain
by Amazon